BI   N

The windo   light as a searchlight   it in its beam and held it. A machine gun opened up, and Ginger flinched as lead lashed the machine like a flail. Splinters flew. He bunched himself into a ball, thinking the undercarriage must be wiped off, as the aircraft swerved sickeningly. This was the end, he thought. Why didn't Voss switch off, the fool. A crash now and they would be in flames.

He breathed again as the Breguet became airborne. A reek of petrol in his nostrils told its own story. Dimly, as in a delirium, he heard Biggles shouting.

Getting up he staggered forward.

BIGGLES – FOREIGN LEGIONNAIRE

CAPTAIN W. E. JOHNS

RED FOX

Red Fox would like to express their grateful thanks for help in
preparing these editions to Jennifer Schofield, co-author of
Biggles: the life of Captain W. E. Johns, published by Veloce
Publications, Linda Shaughnessy of A. P. Watt Ltd and
especially to John Trendler, editor of *Biggles & Co*, the quarterly
magazine for Biggles enthusiasts, the address of which may be
found at the back of the book.

A Red Fox Book
Published by Random House Children's Books
20 Vauxhall Bridge Road, London SW1V 2SA

A division of Random House UK Ltd
London Melbourne Sydney Auckland
Johannesburg and agencies throughout the world

1 3 5 7 9 10 8 6 4 2

First published in Great Britain by
Hodder and Stoughton 1954

Red Fox edition 1995

Phototypeset in Baskerville Roman by Intype, London
Printed and bound in Great Britain by
Cox & Wyman Ltd, Reading, Berkshire

RANDOM HOUSE UK Limited Reg. No. 954009

ISBN 0 09 997980 2

Contents

Chapter 1
Biggles Startles the Chief

'You've been looking unusually preoccupied the last day or two. Something on your mind?' Air-Commodore Raymond, of the Special Air Section, Scotland Yard, put the question to his chief operational pilot casually rather than seriously.

'I've been thinking,' answered Biggles. 'Too much thinking sort of puts a damper on my natural exuberance.'

'Why this sudden mental exertion?' inquired the Air-Commodore, pushing forward the cigarette box.

'Since you ask, I was contemplating putting in a request for six months' leave,' said Biggles calmly.

The Air-Commodore looked startled. 'Six months! Anyone would think you were carrying the world's troubles on your shoulders.'

'Maybe I am,' returned Biggles, reaching for a cigarette.

'So you've decided to take a rest.'

'I didn't say anything about resting. If I do what I have in mind, rest will be a luxury handed out to me in small doses.'

'And just what have you in mind?'

'I'm thinking of joining the French Foreign Legion.'*

* Part of the French army, commanded by French officers, comprising volunteers from all over the world. Formed to serve in the French overseas possessions and with a notorious reputation for brutal training and tough men.

'Now I *know* you need a rest,' declared the Air-Commodore. 'Who gave you this quaint notion, anyway?'

'Marcel Brissac, of the French Sûreté.'

'Is he thinking of joining, too?'

'I believe he's already in.'

The Air-Commodore sat back in his chair and put his fingers together. His manner became serious. 'What's all this about?'

Biggles lit his cigarette and carefully disposed of the match before he answered. 'I had a long talk with Marcel the other day. When he told me that he was going to lose his identity in the Foreign Legion my reactions were the same as yours a moment ago when I suggested doing the same thing. I told him he was crazy. When he gave me his reasons, I was more than ever convinced that he had got a whole hive-full of bees in his bonnet. But as we went on talking a doubt began to creep into my mind. Since then I've been thinking, and doing a little quiet research, with the result that I now believe that Marcel has tumbled to a racket compared with which all other rackets ever organized were mere kid's stuff.'

'That's a tall statement.'

'It may be tall enough to rock the world on its axis if it fell.'

'Why did Marcel pull you into this?'

'Because it concerns us as much as France. In fact, it concerns every country in the world. He realized that he may need help, so, naturally, as we've been working together on the International Police Commission* for some time, he turned to me. I said I'd

---

* An organization with its headquarters in Paris, set up to combat cross-border crime. Frequently known as 'Interpol'.

8

join him if I could get away. Should Marcel disappear, as he feels he may, I would be in a position to carry on from where he left off.'

'You've plenty to do here.'

'What I have to do here is chicken feed compared with what Marcel's tackling—if what he suspects turns out to be fact and not imagination.'

'You'd better tell me about it.'

'All right. But don't start scoffing until I've finished.' Biggles tapped the ash off his cigarette with a slender forefinger. 'Did you notice an item in yesterday's newspapers about a stick of bombs being dropped on some Arabs working near the Israel-Transjordan* frontier?'

'I did.'

'With the result that the treaty which was about to be signed has gone up in flames.'

'Naturally.'

'Have you realized that for years every time two nations at loggerheads have been brought together by the United Nations something of this sort has happened?'

'Now you mention it, yes.'

'And you, like everyone else, have assumed the incident to be an unfortunate accident.'

'In the case you just quoted the Arabs naturally blame Israel or Egypt.'

'They absolutely deny responsibility.'

'It must have been a plane belonging to one or the other.'

'Why must it?'

'Well, as Arabs and Jews have been taking pot shots

---

* Nowadays known as the Hashemite kingdom of Jordan.

at each other for years across a disputed frontier it's a natural assumption.'

'Assumption if you like, but don't talk as if it were an established fact. It's time those who judge these things brought some common-sense to bear. A settlement would suit both sides. Why on earth, then, should either side deliberately kick the apple-cart over?'

'I admit it isn't easy to find a sane reason but that doesn't alter the general opinion as to who was responsible.'

'And that's exactly what was intended. And you, like all the rest, believe it.'

'I do.'

'And I think you're wrong. I believe that neither Egypt, Transjordan nor Israel, had anything to do with it, either by accident or design. I believe they are all as innocent of that attack as you are, although, mark you, it was intended that one of them should take the blame.'

'By whom?'

'By somebody who is interested in keeping the Middle East on the boil. Not only the Middle East. This sort of thing had been happening all over the world wherever a frontier is in dispute. We've seen it happen in South America, Indo-China, North Africa—'

'Just a minute,' broke in the Air-Commodore. 'What are you getting at?'

Biggles's tone of voice took on a quality of deliberation. 'Marcel believes, and I am now convinced, that these trouble-making incidents are not accidents, nor are they designed purely for political propaganda. They're all part of a sinister scheme to kill the efforts of the United Nations to bring about settlement by

10

peaceful means. In other words, someone intends to keep these wars going.'

'Fantastic! For what possible reason?'

'Money. That's the answer, and it sticks out like a sore finger. No—wait a minute. Let me finish. The effect of these incidents is to keep the whole civilized world sweating in a non-stop armaments race—defence programmes, so-called. Every time a truce talk looks like getting somewhere bang goes a bomb and the parley goes to pieces in a cloud of recrimin-ations. As I said just now, this has been going on for years, everybody blaming everybody and the peace-planners getting nowhere. Every time peace looms up the stock markets slump. Every time a bomb goes off, they soar. One bang and up goes the price of oil, rubber, steel and the rest of the basic commodities known as war materials. Somebody is making millions out of this gamble in human lives, and you can't deny it. Would *you* want peace to break out if you were holding millions of pounds' worth of materials and equipment.'

'This is a very serious thing you're saying, Biggle-sworth.'

'I'm aware of it. But it's no use blinking at facts because you don't like the look of them.'

'What facts? So far your argument has been con-jecture.'

'You won't deny that millions are being made out of armaments which sell because no country dare let up on its defence programme.'

'No, I won't deny that.'

'And you won't deny that there are people in the world unscrupulous enough to sabotage peace rather than see wars come to an end?'

The Air-Commodore hesitated.

11

Biggles stubbed his cigarette and took another. 'I told you that I've been doing a little research so I'll give you an example of the sort of cosmopolitan juggler I'm talking about. Julius Rothenburg. Until he died no one had ever heard of him, yet not only was he one of the richest men in the world but one of the most powerful. He could push presidents out of their chairs and throw out any government he didn't like. Yet to this day no one knows where he started life or if Rothenburg was really his name. So close did he keep behind a wall of mystery that no one knew whether he lived in London, Paris, New York, Switzerland or Monte Carlo. He had homes all over the place. Maybe he thought someone would have a crack at him with a gun, which would have been a good thing for the world in general. In the First World War he sold arms to both sides. Between the wars he amused himself by organizing revolutions in South America. His method was to sell arms to one country and then tip off the neighbouring countries that they were about to be attacked. Then they had to buy weapons, too. He never appeared in the picture himself, of course. His deals were put through by a staff manager named Johann Klutz, who was boss of an army of spies—in high places as well as low. It would be interesting to know what Klutz has been doing since Rothenburg died a couple of years ago.'

'You think he may still be in the same line of business?'

'He wouldn't be likely to change—unless, of course, he's retired on his ill-gotten gains. To that sort of man the accumulation of wealth becomes a disease. Gold is their drug. They have to have it.'

'Tell me,' said the Air-Commodore curiously. 'This line of thought started you say with Marcel Brissac?'

'Yes.'

'What put him on to it? Was it just surmise or did some concrete information come his way?'

'I was leading up to that. Yes, it was an accident, a trivial one really, but there were some queer angles to it that set him thinking. It seems that some time ago an aircraft was shot down on the border of French Somaliland. It has just bombed a village on the Abyssinian* side of the frontier. Where it had come from or why it had done such a thing no one could even make a guess; but the result was a riot that nearly started a war.'

'Did this machine carry nationality markings?'

'Yes—and that's the first strange thing about it. The machine was a French type—a Breguet, to be precise—and carried French military insignia. That's what started the fuss. Naturally, Abyssinia blamed France for what looked like an unprovoked outrage. But the Breguet wasn't acting under French orders. What made the thing look bad was, they had to admit ownership of the aircraft. As a matter of fact it had disappeared months before, and had been written off as lost.'

'In what circumstances did it disappear, and from where? I recall the incident and, if I remember rightly the French found it difficult to explain that.'

'Quite true. As a matter of fact, the machine, a light bomber type, on the establishment of Escadrille** 77, serving in North Africa, was taken out of its hangar one night and flown away. You can say it was stolen. Apart from suggesting laxity on the part of the station guards, such a story would have sounded so thin that

* Now Ethiopia.
** French: Squadron.

13

French General Headquarters didn't even put it forward. It wouldn't have been believed if they had. People just don't pinch military aeroplanes from service stations. The French preferred it to be supposed that the machine disappeared while on an official reconnaissance flight. I happen to know, through Marcel, that this was not the first time a machine had disappeared in exactly the same circumstances. I also happen to know that precautions have been taken against a repetition, so should anyone try it again he's likely to get a shock.'

'I see. Carry on.'

'Some time after the Abyssinian incident another bombing attack was made; but this time the French were ready, and had a couple of fighters waiting. When the visitor refused to obey their orders to land they shot him down. The pilot saved his skin by baling out, but was captured. He turned out to be a deserter from the French Foreign Legion—a German named Voss.'

'Wait a minute,' interrupted the Air-Commodore. 'You've got something wrong there. The Foreign Legion has no aviation branch. It would make escape too easy for Legionnaires who decided they didn't like the service after all.'

'I didn't say Voss was *flying* in the Foreign Legion. He was an ordinary foot-slogging soldier. But he could fly. His record showed that he had served in the Luftwaffe under Hitler. Take particular note of that. I'll return to it in a moment. Voss was questioned. Where did he get the machine? What was his object in attacking the village, which was an extraordinary thing to do, and on the face of it, pointless? Well, Voss refused to talk. He said he would be killed if he did, but refused to say by whom. Now note this. While he was

14

awaiting trial Voss contrived to escape in a manner that made it pretty certain he had powerful friends behind him. This wasn't the end. A couple of months later the same man had to make a forced landing in Indo-China* after bombing a friendly village. This time the machine was an American type. Again Voss refused to talk, saying that he would be killed if he did. But the French, who, as you know, take a realist view of this sort of thing, promptly told him he would be killed if he didn't. And to show they weren't kidding they marched him out in front of a firing squad. This made Voss change his mind. Apparently he decided it was better to take a chance than face certain death. So he opened up. He claimed, in the first place, to be a soldier of fortune, prepared to fight anywhere and anybody for the highest bidder. Whilst serving in the Foreign Legion, the only international unit that he knew about, he had been approached by a man who had offered him a lump sum, plus a high rate of pay, if he would desert and enter his service as a pilot. His job would be to obey orders and not ask questions. Once started there could be no changing his mind. If ever he went back on his word he would be killed without mercy. Well, the fellow accepted, and from that time on served in a small cosmopolitan unit based on private air-strips, not shown on any map, in Africa and Asia.'

'Who was the man who induced him to desert?'

'That's what Marcel would very much like to know. The man might be a key to the whole dirty business. But Voss maintained that he didn't know the man. He never heard his name spoken. After he left North

* An area comprising the present day countries of Cambodia, Laos and Vietnam.

15

Africa, where he was serving at the time, he never saw the man again. Marcel doesn't believe that. He's convinced Voss was lying, but he couldn't prove it.'

'Why is he so sure Voss was lying?'

'Because this mysterious recruiting agent must have been aware that Voss was a fully-trained military pilot. How could he know that unless he had seen Voss's records?'

'Voss might have talked about it.'

'It comes to the same thing. If Voss talked about his previous military service it would surely be to his comrades in the Legion. For which reason Marcel believes that Voss knew perfectly well who the man was, because either he must have been in the Legion, or in some way connected with it, to get the information. This hooks up another significant factor. Out of very few desertions from the Legion over the last two years more than half of them had either been pilots or air mechanics. Could that be a coincidence? Marcel doesn't believe it. Neither do I—now.'

'What else did Voss say?'

'Very little, for the simple reason, Marcel thinks, he didn't know much. Voss admitted that although he carried out his orders he never really knew what he was doing, or who he was supposed to be fighting. He received his pay regularly but had no idea who was behind this unit or what its real purpose was. The only man of authority he ever saw was the commandant of the show, another deserter from the Legion known as Capitan Klein. That was all, but the story explained several incidents which up to that time had baffled the Intelligence experts.'

'What finally happened to this fellow Voss?'

'He was tried, got off with a light sentence and has since disappeared.'

16

'And when did Marcel first become suspicious?'

'Some months ago. He began by mustering all the known facts, which told him that Voss's story must be true—at least, in substance. He then had to ask himself what possible purpose a secret military air service could serve. Such an organization would obviously cost a lot of money. Where was the money coming from? People only put up big money when there is a profit hanging to it. Who was getting the profit? At first, he told me, he thought the thing hooked up with fluctuating currency rates of exchange. Watching these put him on to what he believes to be the right track—the international stock markets. It became evident from certain transactions that somebody knew what was going to happen *before it did happen*. Somewhere a smart guy was anticipating every explosion. Shocking though the thought was, it was clear that somebody—and it could only be a financial operator in a big way—was making money by fostering international disunity. Who was it? Well, that's what he's trying to find out, because while it goes on the United Nations are wasting their time. I own the thing seems unbelievable, but there it is.'

The Air-Commodore looked grave. 'If there is anything in this it would certainly explain a lot of things,' he admitted. 'For some time the Foreign Office has been puzzled by the simultaneous appearance of agitators in the unsettled areas. It was plain that they were being financed by someone with a lot of money. In view of what you now tell me I can see that the Foreign Legion, composed largely as it is of men without a country, would be an automatic recruiting centre for a parcel of unscrupulous rogues who put money before loyalty, honour, and every other decent thing.'

17

'That's why Marcel has joined.'

'He's hoping to be recruited as Voss and the others were?'

'He's hoping to get a line on the rat who is organizing these desertions, anyway. He's not worrying about the actual deserters. They're only small fry. He wants to get to the tap-root of the thing.'

'And suppose he does track down the instigator of this monstrous business, what will he do about it? Such a man would have the cleverest legal brains in the world at his command—not that you can arrest a man for making money on the Stock Exchange.'

'Let's catch the fish before we decide what to do with it.'

The Air-Commodore caught Biggles's eye. 'A job in such an organization would just about suit your old opposite number, Erich von Stalhein. I hear his Iron Curtain friends have chucked him out for bungling that Inagua affair*.'

'I hadn't overlooked that possibility,' said Biggles drily. 'I was wondering what had become of him.'

The Air-Commodore got up and paced the floor. 'Of course, if this organization really does exist—and that's such an appalling thought that I'm still reluctant to believe it—there can be no peace in the world until it's buttoned up. If I let you go how are you going to tackle it?'

'Well, it's no use waffling around the world haphazard hoping by a lucky change to spot one of these secret airfields. The alternative is to watch the one place from which we know the organization has drawn

---

* See 'Biggles in the Blue'. See 'Biggles Flies East' (published by Red Fox) for Biggles's first meeting with von Stalhein.

some of its air operatives and mechanics—to say nothing of one or two machines.'

'You mean, you'd join the Legion?'

'Yes, with a specially prepared log-book showing that I'm the sort of man the gang is looking for. That's the bait. If this recruiting agent takes it I should soon hear from him. I'd ask Ginger to come with me— both of us working under assumed names, of course. Bertie and Algy could carry on here unless things should so turn out that I needed extra assistance.'

'Are you going to ask Marcel to lift you into the Legion, to cut out some of the formalities?'

'Not if I can manage without his help. If it were known that I had influential friends I'd be a marked man, and that would probably defeat my object.'

The Air-Commodore returned to his desk. 'I can't say I feel very happy about this,' he muttered.

'Neither do I, if it comes to that,' replied Biggles. 'But apart from the fact that every country in the world is concerned with this affair I feel in duty bound to help Marcel if I can. It may be a long job.'

'It's bound to be a long job,' averred the Air-Commodore. 'You'll have to step slowly, and softly. Some of the big men in international finance have hundreds of men on their pay-rolls, from hotel waiters to high officials. One I could name has an intelligence service as efficient as our own. He has to know what goes on behind the scenes. Fortunately this man is a friend of ours and has more than once given us a useful tip. It's a pity they aren't all like that. Some, the cosmopolitan types, are as ruthless in big business as Hitler was in power politics. One of these may be the man you're looking for. The question is, how are you going to find him.'

'As I said before, I'm hoping he'll find me.'

19

'I see. Is there anything I can do to help?'

'You might let me have a list of that exclusive little coterie of high financiers who buy and sell in millions, yet are so clever in keeping out of the limelight that one never hears their names and seldom see them in print. Photographs of them, if available, would also be helpful.'

'I'll do that,' promised the Air-Commodore.

'Maybe I'll get a line on one of them.'

'See that one doesn't get a line on you,' warned the Air-Commodore, pointedly.

'I'll keep you posted about my movements as often as I can do it with safety,' concluded Biggles, from the door.

Chapter 2
Hard Going

Ginger, standing in the line of shade provided by the barrack-room in which he was quartered, gazed out across a landscape which, if appearance was any guide, had not had its features softened by rain for many a hot North African day. Although the sun had not long started its daily tour across the cloudless dome of heaven it was already lashing the sterile earth with rays unhampered by any trace of humidity.

However, he was glad that he had at last arrived at a station where, if his information was correct, he was likely to stay for some time, for the past five weeks had been a tiresome, troublesome period of movement from London to Paris, Paris to Marseilles, thence to the Foreign Legion Headquarters at Sidi bel Abbes, and now at last to the training-centre near the little town of Zebrit. Life in the Legion was hard, but not as uncomfortable as its reputation had led him to expect.

No obstacle had been put in the way of his, and Biggles's, enlistment, which had been achieved without any 'wirepulling' on the part of Marcel. The reason they had given for wanting to join was the one most common among the men of the several nationalities with whom they had travelled: they wanted a life of action and adventure. In this, the recruiting officer in Paris had assured them, they were not likely to be disappointed. There were no other Britishers in the party during the period of transit.

After the scheme had been approved by the Air-Commodore, Biggles's first step had been to contact Marcel, who made an appointment in Algiers. As ordinary tourists they had flown out, and at the café he had named, talked the matter over. Marcel said he was delighted to have their co-operation, for working on his own he was finding his task tedious, possibly because he had made no progress in his investigations. He didn't know what to do next. His activities were curtailed because, being in the ranks, he had only a few hours off each day. He was really waiting for something to happen. The only person who knew what he was doing was Captain Joudrier of the Sûreté. He had to know, in the same way that Air-Commodore Raymond would have to know.

Biggles agreed that he didn't see how Marcel could do more. To go about asking questions would defeat his object. The same situation would arise in their own case. They could only wait until they were approached by the man who had induced Voss to desert. This, Biggles opined, should not be long if men with flying experience were in fact being recruited from the Legion for the secret air force.

Marcel was anxious to facilitate their enlistment and subsequent progress by a little gentle 'string-pulling' in Paris, through Captain Joudrier. But Biggles would not hear of it, tempting though the offer was. It was too dangerous. The fewer the people who knew what was going on, the better. They would make their own way, even though it was the hard way. When they met, they would pretend not to know each other, so that should one of them slip up the others would not be involved. Meanwhile, for the same reason, there should be no further correspondence between them. Marcel gave them some tips about the procedure of enlistment, and these they found helpful when the time came.

Back in England there had been much to do, getting everything cut and dried down to the last detail. When, finally, they had gone over to Paris, they carried documents which showed that as Flying Officers Biggs and Hepple they had served short-service commissions in the Royal Air Force, being discharged before the expiration of their engagements. These had been accepted without question.

Thereafter everything had gone according to plan until they reached Zebrit. They had hoped to see Marcel at Sidi bel Abbes, but were disappointed. In accordance with their arrangement they refrained from making enquiries for him.

The matter was explained when they reached Zebrit. By then they were afraid that they had lost touch with Marcel altogether, instead of which they found that he was now not only an officer, a sous-lieutenant, but their own company-commander. He had interviewed them briefly on arrival. As the adjutant and a sergeant were present the interview was entirely formal, Marcel giving no sign that he had ever seen them before. Ginger had never seen Biggles so taken aback as he was by this development.

How this strange and unexpected state of affairs had come about they still did not know, for there had been no opportunity to speak to Marcel privately. Biggles was by no means happy about it. He told Ginger he couldn't believe that it was accidental. Marcel had, he was convinced, 'pulled the strings'; and while the new arrangement had obvious advantages it also presented difficulties.

As an officer, Marcel would certainly have greater freedom of movement. He would also be in a position

23

to help them in an emergency. On the other hand, as Biggles pointed out to Ginger when they discussed the matter, contact between them would be much more difficult than if they had all been private soldiers together. This had already been proved. They saw Marcel often enough, of course, but there had been no opportunity to speak to him in private. No doubt Marcel had acted for the best, averred Biggles. There might have been a definite reason for his promotion. He might, thinking it over after he knew Biggles and Ginger were definitely going to join him, have decided that two of them in the ranks was enough, and he would be in a better position to help them if he were an officer. So far they had had no urgent reason to speak to him. The trouble would come when such an occasion arose. At the first opportunity, Biggles said, he would make an assignation with Marcel to arrange a meeting place, possibly a room in the town, where they could discuss their problem.

As things turned out the need for discussion arose before such an arrangement could be made; yet, curiously enough, this apparent failure was to put an important card in their hand.

They had been at Zebrit for a fortnight, still without making contact. Marcel, in passing them on the parade-ground, never gave them a second glance. This, in Biggles's view, was as it should be. Anything looking like intimacy with an officer was bound to lead to a suspicion of favouritism and so incur the rancour of the non-commissioned officers and men with whom they had to share quarters. Marcel would, no doubt, find a way to get in touch with them should he get on the track of anything in the way of a clue. Meantime, there was no point in taking unnecessary risks by speaking to him openly.

Ginger was getting rather bored with it all, although he did not say so. Not that he had any legitimate cause for complaint. Of the alleged brutality in the Foreign Legion he saw nothing. Most of his comrades seemed to be decent enough fellows, although some were 'toughs' that he wouldn't have chosen as companions. This could be said of any military formation. But he found the routine dull, monotonous, tiring and sometimes exhausting. The discipline when on duty was strict. Off duty the legionnaires could do pretty much as they pleased. It was significant, thought Ginger, that a British ex-Tommy* named Graves, who was back at the Depot after being wounded in Indo-China, having completed five years service in the Legion was applying for re-enlistment. No man, he reasoned, would do that if the life was intolerable. What Graves could do, Ginger told himself as he sweated on the interminable route marches, he could do.

For the rest, the company included in its ranks half the nationalities of Europe with a few Africans. Some were displaced persons without a country. There were several Germans who, trained under the Hitler regime, preferred the hard life to a soft job in 'civvy street.' In the next bed to Ginger was a fellow known to everyone as Destin from the fact that in a moment of remorse he had had the word Destin—meaning Fate—tattooed across his forehead. Banished from France for ten years after serving a prison sentence for killing a man in a brawl, he had elected to work out his time in the Legion. Ginger liked him for his cheerfulness and generosity. Whatever the man had

* Popular slang for a British private soldier.

25

been he was now a good soldier, and sincere in his affection for the Regiment.

Ginger's chief worry was the fact that so far nothing had happened to indicate that they were working on the right lines, and time was passing. There was always a chance that they might suddenly find themselves posted to the war in Indo-China, where most of the Legion was serving. He had joined of his own free will, but he didn't want to spend the next five years in it; still less did he relish the idea of finding himself in the thick of a jungle war.

The traitorous recruiting agent, assuming that such a man existed, must have seen their records by now. Why didn't he give a sign that he was aware of their flying experience?

Ginger was about to return to Biggles, whom he had left cleaning his rifle, when a man came strolling towards him. He knew nothing about him except that his name was Voudron, that he was a sergeant in the orderly-room, and spoke French with a curious accent. He was a big, blond, good-looking fellow; but his looks, as far as Ginger was concerned, belied his nature. He was the one man on the station who he really disliked, for not only was his manner harsh and overbearing, but for some reason not apparent he seemed to have picked on them as particular subjects for persecution. It was, Biggles thought, because they were English.

Ginger didn't expect him to stop. Indeed, he hoped he wouldn't; for if he did it would only be to make a remark calculated to irritate him to insubordination. What was Ginger's surprise, therefore, when the sergeant not only stopped, but smiled; and then, to cap all, he offered a cigarette from the popular paper packet.

'*Bon jour, mon camerade,**' greeted Voudron cordially.

'*Bon jour, mon sergent*,' returned Ginger civilly, marvelling at this sudden change of face and wondering what was coming next.

'Tell me, now you have had a taste of it, how do you like it here?' questioned Voudron casually, straightening his cigarette.

'I like it very well,' replied Ginger.

This answer seemed to surprise Voudron. 'After a few marches in the sun, most recruits wish they were anywhere but here,' he averred, smiling.

'It suits me,' stated Ginger simply. 'I was never so fit in my life,' he added, truthfully.

'That's the spirit, *mon enfant.*'

'Why did you ask, monsieur? Do I look miserable?' enquired Ginger.

'*Mais non,*' Voudron hastened to assure him. He hesitated, his eyes on the horizon. 'Me, I would have thought you would have hated this eternal marching after sitting in a comfortable seat, flying an aeroplane.'

Nearly caught off his guard, Ginger felt his muscles stiffen, and he lit his cigarette to hide his face lest it should reveal what was passing in his mind.

Before he could answer Voudron went on: 'You joined with Biggs, didn't you?'

Ginger admitted that this was so.

'You knew each other in the British Air Force, *hein?*'

'*Oui, mon sergent.*'

Voudron half closed an eye knowingly. 'Why did they throw you out before you had finished your time? Oh, you needn't be afraid to tell *me*,' he went on

* French: Good day, friend. Good day, sergeant.

27

breezily. 'Few of us here have always been as good as we might have been.'

Ginger forced a smile, flicking the ash off his cigarette. 'Why talk of the things we come here to forget? I look forward, not back.'

'And so you come to this dust-smitten wilderness to forget, *mon petit*. Me, I would have thought it easier to forget with less discomforture, in the clouds.'

'Perhaps,' answered Ginger, who had resolved to choose his words carefully, and not appear too eager. 'Unfortunately, the clouds are not easy to reach.'

'But a man who can fly aeroplanes can always get work.'

'If his service record is as good as it should be, *mon sergent*. But what is the use of talking about that now?'

'Who knows? The world is full of surprises. But I'll tell you this, my chicken. If I could fly planes I wouldn't be here, sweating for enough francs to buy myself a glass of wine once a week. *La-la*. Wait till you find yourself in the deep desert, my friend, with the sun scorching your eyeballs, and *Le Cafard** eating into your brain. *Alors!* You'll wish you'd gone to prison instead.'

'Since we are talking of this, *mon sergent*, what would *you* do if you could fly planes,' asked Ginger naïvely.

'One day, when I have more time, I'll tell you,' replied Voudron smoothly. 'But I wouldn't burn the soles off my feet for anyone. Nor would I risk being eaten alive by leeches in any jungle.' He half turned to go. 'How about your friend Biggs? Does he like it here?'

---

* *Le Cafard* means literally 'the grasshopper'. A mental disorder induced by heat and lack of amenities.

'You'd better ask him that yourself,' returned Ginger cautiously.

The 'coffee' bugle blew. Voudron tossed the stub of his cigarette away and strode off, leaving Ginger following slowly, but thinking fast. There was plenty to think about. Why this sudden change of face on the part of the sergeant? What was the purpose of his questions? There must have been a purpose, and a definite one. Had he put out a feeler to pave the way for a more concrete suggestion later or was this all part of a recruit's training, to ascertain how he was taking the hard life? These questions would, Ginger did not doubt, be answered in due course. Voudron wouldn't leave the discussion as it stood. He would return to it when his words had had time to sink in.

The significant factor was, Voudron must have seen his papers, and those of Biggles too, or how could he have learned that they had been pilots in the R.A.F.? They had never given a hint of that in public. But, of course, the sergeant was in the orderly-room. He would learn a lot of things there.

Another thought struck Ginger. Had Voudron been trying deliberately to make their lives miserable so that they would be in a receptive mood for suggestions about desertion? Was it for the same reason that he had painted life in the Legion in the worst possible colours? He had certainly done that, and unless it was part of his official duties, that alone made him unfit for the rank he held. Had it not been for that one doubt, that Voudron was testing him officially, Ginger would have been sure that the sergeant was the man they were looking for.

Seeing Biggles walking over to the mess-room he made haste to join him. 'I think I may have struck the trail at last,' he said quietly.

'Good. What's happened?'

'Sergeant Voudron knows we can fly. He must have seen our papers.'

'How did you learn this?'

'He just came over to me as nice as pie and opened up. He as good as said that life in the Legion was purgatory, and wanted to know why, as we were pilots, we had been fools enough to join. You were included.'

'Did he make any definite suggestion?'

'No, but he hinted at desertion. He said he wouldn't stay in the Legion if he could fly.'

'Did he though! That was going a long way. He's over there looking at us now.'

'I don't see that it matters. He must know that I'll tell you what he said. He said nothing about not telling you so he's probably hoping that I will.'

'What was your final impression of his indiscreet conversation?'

'I think he's sown a seed. He'll give it a chance to sprout and then sow some more—that is, unless this morning's quiz happens to be part of his job.'

'I don't think that sort of questioning is part of the programme here or Marcel would have warned us. We can soon settle that.'

'How?'

'By asking Marcel.'

'But how are you going to get in touch with him?'

'I don't know, but we shall have to manage it somehow. An arrangement should have been made before this. I was hoping Marcel would make a move. Presumably he has nothing to say. We'll try to catch him alone in his office; or we may be able to intercept him, and make a signal, as he goes to the officers' mess. But let's get our coffee.'

The opportunity they sought for a word with Marcel

turned out to be even more difficult than they had expected, and the disadvantages arising from their respective positions in the regiment were never more apparent. They could not, of course, simply walk into his office; nor could they request an interview with their commander without giving a reason. Even if they fabricated a reason, Sergeant Voudron, or somebody else, would certainly be present. The officers' mess was out of bounds for everyone except those detailed for duties there. To approach would call attention to themselves, and any hint of association with Marcel was the last thing Biggles wanted, particularly at that moment.

Evening came and they still had not seen him. They were not even sure where he was, but Ginger thought he had seen him enter his office in the administrative building.

'I could find out if he's there,' he told Biggles, becoming tired of waiting.

'How?'

'By walking close past the back window. His office has a window on the far side. Through it I should be able to see his desk.'

'All right. But be careful. Voudron may be watching us. I haven't seen him about for some time. I'll stay here in case Marcel comes out.'

Ginger set off on the walk that would take him to his objective. He did not go direct, but made a detour round the rear of the barracks. There was nothing furtive about the way he did this, for the ground he had to cross was open to all ranks and he had no intention of letting Voudron see him behaving sus-piciously. Actually, as he presently observed, there were two windows. One, he judged from its position, was in Marcel's room, and the other in the general office adjoining it. This turned out to be correct.

Slowing his walk to a saunter, and taking a course as close to the wall as discretion allowed, he came to the first window. He did not stop; nor did he turn his head; his eyes switched, and a single glance in passing revealed the interior of the room. What he saw puzzled him, but a moment later, as he passed the second window, the explanation was forthcoming. It shook him not a little. Lengthening his pace he marched back to where Biggles was waiting.

'Well,' queried Biggles, his eyes on Ginger's face, which was slightly pale under its tan.

'Hold your hat,' muttered Ginger grimly. 'Marcel is in his office, talking on the telephone. Voudron is in the next room, with the communicating door open a crack, listening.'

'I don't like that,' murmured Biggles.

'I thought you wouldn't.'

'That marks our precious sergeant as a snooper, if nothing worse. Let's walk on a little way.' Biggles continued. 'The important thing is, who was Marcel talking to and what was he saying. We shall have to find out. A lot may depend on it.'

'Why not ask Marcel now,' suggested Ginger. 'Here he comes.'

Marcel had left his office and was walking briskly towards the officers' mess on a course that would pass near them.

Biggles's eyes made a swift reconnaissance. The broad parade ground was deserted. 'Voudron may be watching but it's worth a chance,' he decided. 'Behave naturally.'

Marcel came on. They walked towards him, and at a distance of a yard or two came to the salute. 'I must speak,' said Biggles tersely. 'Pretend to tick me off about something.'

Marcel took the cue, pointing at Biggles's unbuttoned tunic with his cane.

Said Biggles, standing to attention. 'Who were you talking to on the 'phone three minutes ago?'

'Joudrier.'

'Voudron was listening. We think he's our man.'

Marcel's face changed colour.

'Where can we talk,' asked Biggles crisply.

'In the town, tonight at nine. In the palm grove behind the Bar Pigale.'

'*Oui, mon commandant*,' said Biggles loudly, seeing Voudron leave his office. He snapped to the salute.

Marcel walked away.

Biggles and Ginger continued on towards their quarters.

Voudron intercepted them. 'What was the commandant talking to you about,' he enquired curiously.

'He choked me off for being improperly dressed,' answered Biggles glibly. 'Nothing is ever right in this infernal place,' he added bitterly. 'I don't mind telling you, *mon sergent*, that there are times when I get a bit tired of it.'

'If I reported you for saying that you'd be for it, Englishman,' asserted Voudron. But he was smiling curiously. 'Don't worry. I'll forget it this time.'

'Thank you, *mon sergent*,' acknowledged Biggles gratefully.

Voudron, still smiling, walked towards the canteen.

Biggles and Ginger went on to the corner where Voudron had spoken to Ginger earlier in the day.

'Let's talk here,' said Biggles shortly.

'Marcel was speaking to Joudrier, of all people.'

'I'd say that's just about torn it as far as Marcel is

concerned,' replied Biggles sadly. 'If Voudron knows Marcel is in touch with the *Sûreté*, and I'm afraid he must, anything can happen. I wonder how long he's been listening to Marcel's phone calls.'

'I'll bet if Marcel goes out tonight Voudron will shadow him.'

'It seems likely. In that case we'll see if we can turn the trick in our favour.'

'How?'

'By following Voudron.'

'With what object?'

'Did you notice Marcel's expression when I told him Voudron had overheard his conversation? I take that to mean he said something important. If I'm right, Voudron's next step will be to pass the information on to the man above him. He may do that by phone, by telegram, or by personal contact if the man is near at hand. We'll see. We're dealing with a gang, remember, not an individual.'

'If Marcel mentioned us by name we've had it as far as the Legion is concerned,' opined Ginger moodily.

'I don't think he could have done, because if he had, Voudron would have avoided us just now, instead of coming over to speak to us. If I'm wrong, it won't merely be a matter of having it as far as the Legion is concerned. If the people we're up against get one sniff that we so much as suspect what's going on they'll make life extremely unpleasant for us. We shall soon know. Thank goodness we've a date with Marcel at last. That's something.'

Chapter 3
The Bar Pigale

The *bistro** known as The Bar Pigale, owned by a stout, jovial Frenchman, known to everyone as Louis, was typical of hundreds of similar establishments to be found in French North Africa. From the outside there was little to recommend it, for it stood in an insalubrious district on the fringe of the *kasbah*—the native quarter. For that reason the rent was low, and this enabled Madame Louis to serve reasonably good food at a price within reach of those who had to work for a living. A rough but sound local wine could be bought for next to nothing the glass, which suited the pockets of the thirsty legionnaires who had to watch their francs carefully.

Another reason for the popularity of the *bistro*, a less worthy one perhaps, was the grove of somewhat bedraggled date palms at the rear of the building, into which, after dark, a soldier might dodge if he had reasons for not wishing to be seen out of camp. The reputation of this retreat, it must be admitted, was not of the best, and sinister tales were whispered of dark deeds that had occurred in it, involving both legionnaires and Arabs, not so long ago. More than one legionnaire, perhaps the worst for drink and with hard-earned pay in his pocket, had gone in never to be seen again, alive or dead. There were old disused wells in the *kasbah*, it was said, that were ideal recep-

* French: bar.

tacles for the disposal of corpses. In a word, like certain quarters of the best European cities, it was a place to be avoided, and inquisitive tourists who ignored warnings did so at their own risk.

These, however, did not apply to the legionnaires, who for the most part were able to take care of themselves, and on occasion found the place useful. Why Marcel had chosen it for a rendezvous was open to guess. He might on the spur of the moment have named the first convenient spot that occurred to him, one which required no directions for locating it. It also had the advantage that being near a common legionnaire resort, there would be nothing in the presence of Biggles and Ginger to call for comment.

They did in fact know the *bistro* well, having called more than once to quench their thirst in the course of their off-duty walks.

With plenty of time on their hands before the hour appointed for the meeting with Marcel, Biggles decided to employ it rather than hang about without any definite purpose; so leaving the barracks, which were some little distance from the town, shortly after seven, they went only part of the way. Finding a place to sit in the inky shadow of a tall cactus hedge, from where they could watch the road without being seen, they settled down to wait. If Voudron passed they would see him, and watch where he went.

It was a beautiful night, hot and windless, with a moon, nearly full, making the scene a picture of pale blue light and hard black shadows. Crickets kept up a continual chirping, making an astonishing amount of noise for insects so small. Some distance away, from a pool or irrigation ditch, came the automatic croaking of a bull-frog.

Some Arab workmen trudged wearily home from

where they had been working in a vineyard. Others passed with donkeys carrying bundles of firewood or forage. Legionnaires passed in twos and threes, laughing or grumbling as the case might be, to spend the evening in the town. Ginger, quite comfortable, little suspecting what the night held in store for them, was in no hurry to move.

The end came when they had been there about an hour. A single tall figure in uniform came striding down the road, his boots scraping harshly on the gravel.

'Voudron,' whispered Biggles.

They sat motionless while he went past.

Biggles gave him a good start, but without losing sight of him, and set off in pursuit. 'He's nervous,' he told Ginger. 'He wouldn't be sweating along at that rate if he hadn't something on his mind. We'll keep to the side of the road although it doesn't matter if he sees us. He'd hardly recognize us at this distance and there are still fellows from the camp going to and fro.'

Keeping the sergeant in sight they walked on, keeping the same gap between them until they reached the outskirts of the town, where the residential quarter began, when Biggles closed the distance somewhat rather than risk losing his man among other pedestrians. On both sides now were pillars carrying decorative wrought-iron gates that gave access to short drives bordered by sub-tropical gardens. Behind were the white-painted villas, with shuttered windows, of the more well-to-do residents. Palms, with graceful arching fronds, threw lace-like patterns on the walls and across the dusty road.

Suddenly the figure in front disappeared.

'He must have turned in somewhere,' said Biggles hurrying forward.

Reaching the spot where they had last seen the sergeant they stood still, and listening, located his footsteps retreating up a gravel drive. Looking through the open ironwork of the gate they were just in time to see him enter the arched porchway of the front door of a villa. A moment later a patch of yellow light streamed across the drive as the door was opened to admit him.

'So our two-faced sergeant has friends in big houses,' murmured Biggles. 'Very useful for him and very interesting to us.' Taking a pace back he read the name of the house. 'Villa Mimosa.' He then advanced to one of the white gate-posts on which, as is common in France, a brass plate announced the name and profession of the occupier. 'Jules Raban. *Avocat*,' he read softly. 'What does Voudron want with a lawyer, I wonder?' He looked at his watch. 'Maybe we can find out. We have plenty of time.' He glanced up and down the road. 'Okay,' he whispered. 'Come on—quiet.'

The gate opened to his touch. They went in, closing it noiselessly behind them. Two steps took them to a fringe of soft earth sparsely planted with exotic shrubs. Along this they made their way to the house. At a distance of a few yards Biggles stopped to make a reconnaissance.

The drive lay white in the moonlight, with shadows sprawling across it like pools of ink. Through the slatted shutters of a window on the ground floor, not fully closed, alternate bars of yellow and black showed that the room was lighted. The only sound was the brittle chirping of a cricket in a nearby palm.

Motioning Ginger to follow Biggles moved on to a

38

position from which they would be able to see the interior of the room.

What Ginger saw did not surprise him. Standing by a table laid for dinner, as if he had just risen from his meal, was a short, dark, stout man, immaculately dressed, presumably the lawyer. Just inside the door, holding out his hands apologetically as though to excuse himself for the intrusion, but talking volubly, was Sergeant Voudron. Unfortunately the window itself was closed, so no sound reached the outside. But it was clear from the intent expression on the face of the listener that Voudron had startled him. At this juncture, as if he realized suddenly that they might be overlooked, the dark man crossed the room swiftly and drew the curtains. Somewhere in the house a bell jangled.

Biggles looked at Ginger. 'Pity about that. No matter. We saw enough to confirm our belief. We shall see nothing more so we might as well get out while the going's good.'

Actually, the going was not quite as good as Biggles supposed, for as they neared the gate, keeping of course in deep shadow, happening to glance over his shoulder Ginger saw a man advancing quickly down the drive. A warning touch on Biggles's arm sent them both crouching behind a bush. The man passed within five yards but did not see them. He went straight to the gate. For a moment the moonlight fell on the head and shoulders of a massively-built black man. A key scraped in a lock. To lock the gate had obviously been his task, for turning about he walked back to the house and disappeared from sight.

'We're locked in,' observed Ginger.

'That needn't worry us. We'll go out over the wall.

Clearly, Monsieur Raban doesn't want any more visitors tonight.'

To scale the wall was a simple operation and a minute later they were on the road, brushing dust from their hands and tunics.

'That little effort was well worth while,' remarked Biggles. 'I fancy we know from whom our tricky sergeant gets his orders.'

'And now what?'

Again Biggles looked at his watch. 'We've still got forty minutes in hand. We'll wait a little while to see how long Voudron stays, and if possible check where he goes when he comes out.'

They had to wait for twenty minutes before Voudron reappeared. At the precise moment that the black man was unlocking the gate for him who should come along but Marcel, although this, in view of his appointment, was natural enough. The two men at the gate stood like statues. Marcel went past without noticing them. Biggles dare not reveal himself with Voudron so close, so unaware that he was the target for four pairs of eyes Marcel went on towards the town.

Voudron gave him a start of about forty yards and then took the same direction. He must have recognized Marcel, although whether he was actually following him, or intended going into the town anyway, was not clear.

Biggles gave Voudron a couple of minutes and then he, too, followed on.

To Ginger there was nothing remarkable about the situation. It was, or seemed, a perfectly natural one, due to the sequence of events. He knew what Marcel was doing. He knew what they themselves were doing. What Voudron had in mind he did not know, of course, but it didn't occur to him that it was anything out of the ordinary. So he merely hoped that Voudron wouldn't get in their way.

They could no longer see Marcel, for he was now some distance ahead, and as the number of people moving about, many of them legionnaires, increased as they neared the town, it was not easy to keep Voudron in sight. Wherefore Biggles improved his pace, remarking: 'It looks as if he's going to the Pigale too, confound him. We don't want him to see us talking to Marcel.'

By this time they were close to the *bistro*, which, as has been narrated, was near the native quarter. Not only was there a number of Arabs moving about, as might have been expected, but several legionnaires, making for the popular rendezvous. The circumstance that they all wore the same uniform made identification difficult except from a short distance. The result of this was almost inevitable.

'I can't see either Marcel or Voudron,' asserted Ginger.

'Have you any idea which way Voudron went?'

'He didn't go into the bar, so I think he must have gone into the *kasbah*.'

'That seems most unlikely. What would he want there at this time of night? If he has, it's no use trying to find him in that rabbit warren. What happened to Marcel, anyway? It's still too early for the appointment. Ten to nine.'

'He must have gone into the Pigale to wait for nine o'clock.'

'Let's see.'

They went on to the bar, a confused babble of voices meeting them at the open door. Through a haze of pungent tobacco smoke they could see Marcel talking to the proprietor. He saw them enter but gave no sign of recognition.

'He probably looked in to see if we were here before going into the grove,' Biggles told Ginger, looking round. 'I don't see Voudron so goodness knows where he went. Perhaps it doesn't matter. He's not likely to be in the grove. There's no need for us to stay in this fug. Let's get outside. We'll see Marcel when he leaves.'

Leaving the *bistro* they took up a position in a narrow archway on the opposite side of the road, from where they would see Marcel when he emerged; and they had only been there a few moments when Ginger caught Biggles by the arm. 'There's Voudron,' he said tersely. 'Just coming out of the *kasbah* with two Arabs.'

'What's he doing with that nasty-looking pair of cutthroats?' muttered Biggles.

Watching, they saw the sergeant, followed closely by the two Arabs, walk to a nearby doorway and take up positions as if they, too, were watching the Bar Pigale.

'What goes on?' breathed Ginger. 'There's something about this set-up I don't like.'

They did not have to wait long for the answer. Marcel appeared, and walked towards the grove with the obvious intention of keeping the appointment. This brought a frown to Biggles's forehead, for the awkward position arose that they could not move without being seen by Voudron. But the situation was saved when the two Arabs followed Marcel, and Voudron, crossing the road, went into the Pigale. Biggles at once set off after Marcel, and the Arabs who were obviously following him.

Not for a moment did it occur to Ginger that the

Arabs were trailing Marcel with the intention of doing him bodily harm. He thought Voudron had merely set them to watch him, and the question at once arose, how were they to have a conversation with Marcel without having the matter reported to the sergeant? In the event, however, the problem solved itself. Instead, they were presently involved in a situation much more alarming.

Neither he nor Biggles had ever actually been inside the grove, having had no occasion to go that way; but they knew where it was. They also knew that its real purpose was what it had always been; to provide shade and a rough grazing ground for the goats and donkeys belonging to the Arabs in the *kasbah*. They were well aware of its ugly reputation, of course, for it had often been discussed in barracks. Destin had several times warned them to keep clear of it. Fights between legionnaires had occurred there so often in the past that there had been talk of putting it out of bounds; but this had come to nothing, following the general practice of allowing the troops to do as they pleased in their own time.

The place turned out to be not so large as they had expected, covering, as far as they could judge in the moonlight, about an acre of ground. It was neither a pretty nor pleasant place, considered from any angle. It was simply an area of waste ground from which rose a stand of ancient date palms. There was no undergrowth or herbage. The palms sprang straight from the dusty earth. Aside from anything else the place stank to high heaven, and this alone would have discouraged Ginger from entering had he no particular reason for doing so.

It was dark under the trees, although here and there slants of moonlight, casting fantastic shadows

43

on the sand, did no more than enhance the sinister atmosphere of the place. A sultry, unhealthy hush hung in the stagnant air.

At first they could see no one, neither Marcel nor the Arabs, although they knew they must be there. In the ordinary way Biggles would have whistled, but the circumstances demanded silence. Then, as they stood there, eyes probing the gloom, hesitating to advance, a match flared, and they saw Marcel standing under a palm a short distance away in the act of lighting a cigarette. That he was waiting for them was evident.

But still for a moment Biggles did not reveal himself. He stood staring into the grotesque shadows, first on one side then the other. Ginger knew what he was looking for. Where were the Arabs? There was still no reason to suppose that they intended any physical harm. But they were obviously acting as spies for Voudron, and Biggles dare not take the risk of having a clandestine meeting with Marcel reported; for should the sergeant learn that they had met Marcel by appointment he could hardly fail to draw correct conclusions.

Ginger, too, was staring. A movement caught his eye. Had a shadow flitted across a patch of moonlight about twenty yards from the tree against which Marcel stood? He wasn't sure. He focused his eyes on the spot. Another ghostlike figure followed the first— swift, silent, furtive.

Without moving his eyes Ginger touched Biggles and pointed. He was still not sure what it was he had seen. He had not forgotten that the place was used by animals. Even if the vague shapes he had seen were men there was no indication that they were not on business of their own, for, after all, the grove was public property. But he could not shake off a feeling that something felonious was going on.

But when he made out two figures creeping towards the tree against which Marcel stood all doubts were banished, and the truth struck him like a ton of bricks, as the saying is. Moonlight glinting on an object in the hand of one of the men confirmed his worst fears, and the warning cry that broke from his lips was instinctive rather than calculated.

'*Prenez garde, commandant,** he cried shrilly, and darted forward.

* French: Look out, commandant.

Chapter 4
Something to Think About

The Arabs reached the tree first. Steel flashed. Marcel, who had jumped clear of it, lashed out with the swagger cane* he carried. Then Biggles and Ginger arrived on the scene with a rush. Even so, the Arabs were not prepared to abandon their onset, which concentrated on Marcel.

Neither Biggles nor Ginger carried a weapon of any sort. Marcel apparently had only his light cane. The Arabs had daggers, ugly curved blades which they knew how to use. Ginger darted in behind the nearer, who was pressing Marcel hard, and slammed home a fist in a vicious kidney punch that brought a gasp to the man's lips. Marcel lashed him across the face. Biggles tripped the other, and before the man could recover knocked him flat and then stamped on the hand that held the dagger. Deprived of his weapon the Arab scrambled up and bolted. His companion, seeing him go, followed. In a moment they were lost to sight in the intricate pattern of the palms and their shadows.

No attempt was made to pursue them. The attack had failed in its purpose, which, clearly, was murder, and that was all that mattered. To follow the men into the honeycomb of the *kasbah* would have been suicidal, as they were all aware, wherefore, breathing

---

* A short cane or stick carried by officers when walking out.

heavily from shock and exertion, they looked at each other while they recovered their breath.

'Name of a dog!' panted Marcel. 'What happens?'

'Those two rascals were out to get you, and it wasn't just robbery they intended,' Biggles told him seriously. 'Voudron put them on to you. He fetched them from the *kasbah*. We happened to be watching. They stalked you. We stalked them. You're a marked man, so watch your step.' After a swift glance round he went on: 'Why did you ring Joudrier?'

'I didn't. He rang me from Paris.'

'What did you say? Voudron must have heard every word.

'He merely rang up to find out how I was getting on, and to ask if there was anything he could do.'

'Did you mention us by name?'

'No.'

Biggles gave a little sigh of relief. 'That's something, anyway.'

'What do you know about Voudron,' asked Marcel.

'He's spoken to Ginger about flying. He's seen our records. He didn't make any suggestion about desertion but he paved the way for it. He's the monkey in the woodpile here. His eavesdropping pretty well confirmed it. This last affair, the object of which was murder, proves it. He knows what you're doing here, and tonight he was ordered to liquidate you.'

'By whom?'

'I have reason to believe by a lawyer named Jules Raban, who lives at the Villa Mimosa. We watched Voudron go to the villa an hour or so ago. We saw him talking to Raban. Afterwards he went to the *kasbah* and produced those two thugs. Raban is in the ring; we needn't doubt that; and he's put you on the spot, so my advice is carry a gun and keep out

47

of dark corners. Get Joudrier to find out all he can about Raban. He may have a police record.'

'But what about Voudron. Shall I—'

'Leave him alone. Let him carry on. He'll lead us—'

'Watch out!' broke in Ginger tersely. 'Here he comes.'

'Let us know how and where we can report developments,' Biggles told Marcel under his breath. 'We must have a line of communication.'

There was no time for more. Nor was it possible to leave the grove without being seen by Voudron, who was already close and coming towards them.

He strode up. 'Has there been trouble here, *mon commandant?*' he enquired, looking from one to the other.

Biggles answered. '*Monsieur le commandant* was attacked by Arab thieves. We were walking past the grove and heard a cry for help. Rushing in we saw the commandant being attacked by two Arabs. When we went for them they ran. That's all.'

'Is anyone hurt?'

'No.'

'*Mot de Cambronne!*' exclaimed Voudron. 'It comes to something when this *kasbah* scum dares to attack an officer. I, too, heard someone call out, just as I was leaving the Pigale, so I came to investigate; but in the dark for a time I could see nothing.'

Ginger smiled at this glib explanation, which was a palpable lie. Voudron was either looking for Marcel's body, or had been told by the Arabs that the attack had failed.

'I would say,' went on Biggles thoughtfully, 'that in the darkness those Arabs didn't see that the man they intended to rob was an officer. More likely they thought it was some fellow who had been behaving as if he had money in his pocket.'

'True,' agreed the sergeant. 'All the same, it's time this stinking hole was laid flat. It has always been a hide-out for thieves and cut-throats.' He turned to Biggles and Ginger. 'If you take my advice you'll get back to barracks and stay there. Those Arabs may have seen your faces. If so, as you made enemies of them, they'll be after your blood.'

'Yes, sergeant,' agreed Biggles obediently.

Voudron spoke to Marcel. 'I'd better walk back to the camp with you, monsieur, in case those devils are still hanging about.'

'I don't need an escort,' answered Marcel stiffly. '*Bon soir**.' He walked away.

The others strolled on to the road. 'Are you coming home with us, sergeant?' enquired Biggles innocently.

'No. I'm not going back just yet,' answered Voudron. 'I've got a date with my girl,' he explained, as if he felt that an explanation was necessary.

'*Entendu***,' replied Biggles. 'We'll get along. *Bon soir, mon sergent.*' So saying, with Ginger by his side, he set off up the road towards the barracks.

They walked a little way in silence. Then Ginger said: 'That was a nice how-do-you-do. Voudron apparently thinks nothing of murder. As a type he's even lower down the scale than I thought.'

'The whole picture is now pretty plain,' returned Biggles. 'Voudron, having heard Marcel talking to the Sûreté, must know he's a police spy put in for a purpose; and a guilty conscience will probably tell him what that purpose is. As soon as he could get

* French: Good evening.
**French: I see.

49

away he went and reported his discovery to Raban, whom we may suppose is the local member of the gang from whom he takes his orders. Raban must have told Voudron to deal with Marcel, whereupon he went to the *kasbah* and hired a brace of Arabs to do the dirty work. From the fact that he knew just where to find them at short notice I suspect he's employed them before. At all events, he must be known in the *kasbah* or he wouldn't dare to go in after dark. I don't know any *kasbah* anywhere that's really safe for a white man after dark. The Arabs must have been delighted to see Marcel go into the grove. That made the job simple. Otherwise they would have knifed him on the road back to the camp, no doubt. They may have wondered why he went into the grove but they couldn't have known it was to keep an appointment with us, so that leaves us in the clear.'

'Voudron was hanging about to hear if his thugs had done the job.'

'Of course he was. Now, I imagine, he's gone to them to find out exactly what happened. I don't think that need worry us. It could all have happened just as we said. There was nothing extraordinary about us being near the grove. If we saw an officer being attacked, or a comrade for that matter, we should naturally go to his assistance. Voudron has absolutely no reason to suppose we had an appointment with Marcel. Incidentally, it was lucky for Marcel that we were dead on time, or he'd have had it. The unfortunate part about the whole thing is, his connection with the police will soon be known to the gang for whom Voudron is working, and that puts him out of the business as far as his usefulness here is concerned. If he isn't very careful he'll end up in one of those old wells in the *kasbah*. Voudron will have to tell Raban that the attempt to murder him failed because a couple of stray legionnaires happened to come along. Raban's reply to that will be to tell him to try again, and keep on trying until he succeeds. For which reasons I shall advise Marcel at the first opportunity to pack up and have himself sent back to Paris. Joudrier will be able to organize that, of course.'

'If the gang suspects what Marcel was doing here they'll know their racket has been rumbled, and even if Marcel goes back to Paris they'll be on the watch for others on the same job.'

'I'm afraid you're right. They'll tighten things up. We shall have to go warily. The gang is clever, ruthless and efficient, and even now we may not guess how far its ramifications extend. We shan't be able to trust a soul. What we've seen so far is proof of that.'

'But we're still in the clear.'

'I think so. In a show like this one can never be sure, though. We shall soon know. The way Voudron behaves tomorrow may tell us.'

They walked on up the moonlit road towards the camp.

Chapter 5

Sergeant Voudron Opens Up

The next two days passed without incident. The dull routine of drill and route marches went on, giving Ginger a curious feeling that he was living two lives, one as a soldier and the other as—well, he didn't know quite what. His normal life in London began to seem remote. When he thought of Algy and Bertie it was as if they were in another world—which in some respects they were.

They saw Marcel frequently. He made no attempt to speak to them, nor did they approach him. He had apparently decided to carry on, regardless of the perilous position in which the unfortunate telephone conversation with the Sûreté had placed him. Voudron, too, was often about, both on and off the parade-ground. His manner was curt, but not exactly unfriendly. Not once did he refer to the affair in the grove. As far as he was concerned it might never have happened. More than once they watched for him to leave the camp, but if he went out they did not see him go. It seemed as if he, too, was being careful.

In a word, it was as if a sudden storm had passed, leaving everything tranquil. But Ginger was not deceived. This calm, he felt, was false, and would not persist for long. What form the next storm would take he did not know, but that it would come he felt sure. In particular he was uneasy on Marcel's account.

On the morning of the third day Biggles received a letter through the post. The address was typewritten, and until he opened it he had no idea of whom it was from. The envelope yielded a single flimsy sheet of paper. There was no address or superscription. The message consisted of one paragraph, also typed. It was signed with the solitary letter M. But the context explained everything.

Biggles read the letter and handed it to Ginger without a word.

'The name of the man in whom you are interested is an alias,' read Ginger. 'Formerly a criminal lawyer in Paris he left after the war on being denounced as a collaborator during the Occupation. He then went to Marseilles where he assumed his present name and practised successfully as a defence counsel in shady cases. He defended, among others, a man named Voss. He has offices at Tangier and Casablanca and travels from one to the other. Present address is his country home during the heat of Summer. M.'

Ginger passed the letter back to Biggles who put a match to it and reduced it to ashes.

'So that's Monsieur Raban,' murmured Biggles. 'He defended Voss, the deserter, who flew for the gang. We needn't be surprised at that. His offices are, I imagine, merely a cover for more lucrative trans-actions. The gang would have lawyers and he's one of them—a step higher up the ladder than Voudron. We'll keep an eye on his villa in our spare time. The snag is, we don't get enough spare time. The villa should be watched constantly, both for visitors and to see where he goes when he makes excursions. That might lead us to the next man above him. We're still only at the bottom of the ladder.'

'Why not get Algy over to watch him? I mean, as an ordinary tourist.'

'That's an idea,' agreed Biggles. 'I'll think about it.'

This was only the beginning of what was to prove an eventful day.

The next thing to happen was the circulation of a rumour in the camp, in the mysterious way such rumours occur in all military establishments, that a draft was to be sent to Fort Labougant. No one knew where the rumour started, and Ginger, who at first was quite disinterested, was puzzled by the buzz of excitement it produced. The explanation was forthcoming. It was provided by some of the old hands who knew the place from personal experience. Others had heard of it.

It was, from all accounts, the most deadly outpost for which the Legion provided the garrison. Deep in the Sahara, it was, according to those who knew, the nearest place to hell on earth. The heat, the glare and the hideous loneliness, had to be experienced to be believed. More men went out of their minds with *Le Cafard* at Fort Labougant than all the other stations put together.

Naturally, the great matter for speculation was the names of those most likely to be drafted. Some there were who declared that they would shoot themselves rather than face this dreadful ordeal. Others swore they would desert first. To these wild threats Biggles and Ginger listened with quiet amusement, knowing that it was all talk, and that in the event none of the speakers would do anything of the sort. They themselves were not concerned. Not having completed their training it did not occur to either of them that their names might be on the fateful list.

But the next rumour that flew, a little while later, brought an expression of alarm to Biggles's face. It was that Sous-Lieutenant Brissac was to conduct the draft and take over the command of the Fort.

Biggles looked at Ginger. 'I don't like the sound of that. I wonder . . .'

'Wonder what?'

'If there's more in it than meets the eye.'

'You mean—has somebody been pulling the strings to put Marcel out of the way?'

'Yes. He might as well be dead as be stuck in the middle of the Sahara.'

'But only the higher command could order such a posting.'

'Maybe there's someone in the gang powerful enough to give orders to the higher command.'

Ginger stared.

'I mean that,' asserted Biggles. 'We're not dealing with a bunch of cheap swindlers. This time we're up against something big—bigger even than we may suppose even now.'

'Marcel will refuse to go. He'll resign his commission and the Sûreté will see that his resignation is accepted.'

'Of course he'll resign—and that will tell the enemy what they may wish to confirm. That Marcel is a police agent, and the police are at last wise to the armaments racket. Apart from that, don't you see that whether Marcel goes to Fort Labougant or whether he resigns, he'll be out of the business and we shall be left here on our own. Of course he can't go to the Fort, but if he resigns it won't take the enemy intelligence service very long to find out why he was permitted to walk out of the Legion.'

Said Ginger, whimsically: 'Well, thank goodness they don't suspect us, or we may find ourselves on the way to Fort Labougant, too.'

Still talking, wondering what course Marcel would take, but not unduly disturbed, they went outside. Voudron was walking across the square. Seeing them, he changed direction and came over to them.

'If the Arabs are going to get you for what you did the other night they'll have to be quick,' he said cheerfully.

'How so?' enquired Biggles.

'You're on the draft for Fort Labougant.'

'Both of us?'

'Yes.'

Biggles's expression did not change. 'How do you know? Have you seen the list?'

'Seen it? I helped to make it up. Why do you think I'm in the orderly-room?'

'And why did you choose us for this honour?' queried Biggles.

'Well, in the first place you said you liked the life, so I thought I'd give you a chance to see what real soldiering is like. Then again, thinking of those spiteful Arabs I thought you'd be safer away from here.' Voudron spoke casually. Then he dropped his voice. 'Of course, you needn't go if you don't want to.'

'What exactly do you mean by that,' asked Biggles slowly.

'Come over here,' answered the sergeant, inclining his head towards a solitary palm near the edge of the square where there was no possibility of being overheard.

'Well now, here we are,' said Voudron, vaguely.

Ginger had a strong suspicion of what was coming, but there was still much that he did not guess. He thought Marcel's name might be mentioned, and if so, the way Voudron introduced it would be interesting. For the moment, however, the sergeant seemed to be uncertain how to start. He offered his cigarette packet and lit one himself.

Biggles helped him by taking the initiative. '*Alors, mon sergent**,' said he. 'Suppose we stop talking in riddles. You say we are going to Fort Labougant. You say also that we needn't go if we don't want to. How can we, or you, prevent it?'

Voudron still seemed loath to commit himself. He made a gesture as if he was not really serious. 'I was merely thinking of what others have done, and what I myself might do were I in your position.'

'And what would you do,' asked Biggles.

'I might take a walk and forget to come back.'

'Are you suggesting that we desert the regiment?'

Voudron grimaced. 'Me, I don't like this word desert. Let us say you could take a holiday without asking permission.'

'Forgive me, sergeant, if I ask an embarrassing question. But we are all men of the world, and as we know, there is no taste in nothing. What good would it do you if we decided not to go to Fort Labougant?'

'Don't let that worry you, *mon enfant*. It's my nature to help people when they're in trouble.'

Biggles, of course, was trying to make it easier for Voudron to come to the point; for this was what he had been waiting for, what he had hoped would happen.

'Very well,' he said. 'Let us admit that we don't

* French: So, Sergeant.

57

want to go to Fort Labougant. Let us admit that rather than do that we would be prepared to—er—take a walk. Now, you know the ropes. How do we go? Where do we go? And what could we do to save ourselves from starvation?'

'One thing at a time,' protested Voudron. 'I admit I have friends who might be willing to help you. For example, would you like to go on flying aeroplanes.'

'Of course.'

'And if I could get you such a job would you take it?'

'But certainly.'

'Without asking questions?'

'A man in his right mind doesn't argue with his bread and butter,' said Biggles tritely. 'But allow me to say this without offence. I find it hard to believe that you could arrange this for us.'

'Naturally,' conceded Voudron. 'But I assure you that I can. Now I must say this.' The smile remained on his face but there was no humour in his eyes. 'If you repeat one word of this conversation to anyone you might get certain people into trouble, and as they are people with influence the result might be unfortunate for you.'

'As if we should do such a thing,' protested Biggles.

'One never knows and I have to be careful.'

'Obviously. What about this job? Where is it?'

'You will learn that later. All I can say now is, it is a long way from here, which should suit you.'

'And how would we go?'

'In an aeroplane. That would be arranged for you. But already you ask too many questions. In any case we had better not stand here talking any longer. You are definite you will go?'

'Absolutely.'

'Very well. We will talk more of this presently, but not here. Meet me tonight at seven o'clock just past the ruined mosque on the way to the town.'

'*Bien entendu**.'

Voudron turned away and strode off across the square.

They watched him go. 'What a rat. What a snake in the grass,' sneered Ginger.

'Don't grumble. He's taking us where we want to go.'

'I've pictured myself as a lot of things, but never as a deserter,' said Ginger bitterly.

'That's what we came here for, isn't it? The next thing is to find Marcel and tell him what we're doing. I must also write some letters.'

'Aren't you shattered by all this?'

'Not particularly. It's happened before. You can see that from the way Voudron had everything worked out. Breaking the ice with us without committing himself too deeply was his most difficult task. Well, he's done that. Now he'll go ahead. By thunder! Marcel certainly struck something when he hit the trail of this outfit. We'd better do something about getting in touch with him. Voudron has gone into the canteen. That may give us a chance.'

'You're going to keep this appointment with him?'

'You bet I am. I—'

'There's Marcel now,' broke in Ginger urgently. 'Standing talking to the adjutant. With Voudron in the canteen this is our chance. If we walk past Marcel and go into the rear of the building he'll guess we want to speak to him.'

'I think you're right,' agreed Biggles. 'We can't do

---

* French: That's understood.

Marcel any harm, anyway, since Voudron has got him taped. Let's go.'

They marched briskly across the parade-ground, and without checking their stride, saluted in passing. Biggles chose to pass on the side behind the adjutant, which enabled him to catch Marcel's eye significantly. They went straight on to the rear of the station head-quarters. There they waited, and presently had the satisfaction of seeing Marcel come round the corner and walk towards them.

'Listen, Marcel,' began Biggles without preamble. 'Things are moving fast. This posting of ours to Fort Labougant gave Voudron the opportunity to come into the open.'

Marcel was staring. 'Fort Labougant? What are you talking about?'

'We've been drafted to Fort Labougant—haven't we?'

'Nonsense!'

'Haven't you been posted there too?'

'Certainly not.'

It was Biggles's turn to stare. 'But . . . but . . . Voud-ron told us we were on the draft.'

'He's a liar.'

'But he said he made out the list.'

'*Encore**, I repeat, he's a liar. There is no such draft, or even a suggestion of one.'

Understanding dawned in Biggles's eyes. 'So that's it,' he breathed. 'I get it. That crafty rogue started the rumour himself, and then, pretending it was in confidence tipped us off that we were on the draft. That was to get us into the mood to desert. I must confess he took me in, the scheming hound.'

* French: again.

'Has he actually suggested that you desert?'

'Yes.'

Marcel went white. His nostrils quivered with passion. '*Mon Dieu*! I'll have the rascal put—'

'Do nothing,' Biggles implored him quickly. 'Things go well. We're meeting him tonight to settle the details. I'll let you know what happens, but you'd better be prepared for our sudden disappearance. Voudron has offered to get us a job, flying, and he may want us to go very soon. Meanwhile, you watch your step. Things are getting warm, and with Voudron and his gang murder is all part of the day's work. That's enough for now. We'll move off in case Voudron should see us together.'

'If he offers you this job you'll desert, and take it?'

'Of course. That was the purpose of our coming here.'

Marcel shook his head. 'I don't like it. I must think. I will go now.' Looking worried he walked away.

Biggles and Ginger went off in the opposite direction.

'That cunning, crafty crook,' grated Ginger, apparently still thinking of the way Voudron had tricked them.

'He may be all that, and more,' returned Biggles evenly. 'But the man isn't a fool. That was a clever move on his part. Had Marcel not been an officer we might never have known the truth about this imaginary draft. Had we been staying on here we should have known eventually, of course; from which we may take it that Voudron doesn't expect us to be here much longer. Be careful not to let it out that we know this draft talk to be without foundation.'

Chapter 6

'Everything Has Been Arranged?'

When Biggles told Marcel that Voudron might want them to go fairly soon if they accepted his proposition, he was thinking of days, and possibly weeks, rather than hours. He assumed that it would take some time to complete the arrangements. As he admitted later to Ginger, in spite of all he had said about the efficiency of the organization to whom they were opposed, he had still under-estimated the power and scope of it.

He wrote a note to Algy, and a concise letter to the Air-Commodore, reporting progress, putting both in the same envelope and addressing it in an illiterate hand-writing to their London apartment. He did not entirely trust the post, thinking it within the bounds of possibility that the enemy exercised some sort of censorship on the mail of legionnaires with whom they were in touch; but the risk had to be taken. He felt—for their own sakes apart from anything else—that he couldn't leave his headquarters in complete ignorance of what had happened should they disappear without trace. He posted the letter himself at the general post office in the town, Ginger shadowing him to check that he was not being shadowed. This done they set off back up the road towards the camp to keep the appointment with Voudron.

The sergeant arrived at the ruined mosque on time

and greeted them cordially. 'I see you haven't changed your minds,' he said.

'We should be fools to miss such a chance as this,' returned Biggles.

'You're quite right,' answered Voudron. 'If you do what you're told this may be the making of you—a different matter from rotting your brains at Fort Labougant.'

'These friends of yours must be useful people to know,' ventured Biggles.

'They are.'

'But how do you come out of this. I feel we owe you something for this service.'

'Forget it. Anything to oblige two decent fellows like you. I'm not short of money; nor will you be from now on, as you'll see for yourselves presently.'

'What do you mean by that?'

'Your pay will start right away.'

'Do you mean you're going to pay us?'

'Me? No. My friend will pay you. You're going to meet him.'

'Tonight?'

'Right now. See, he's even sent his car along for us.'

A sleek shining American car had slid silently to a stop at the side of the road. The driver got out to open the door for them. Ginger recognized the big man who had locked the gate at the Villa Mimosa, so he knew where they were going. This caused him no surprise. The Villa Mimosa was obviously the first step in the line of communication to their ultimate objective.

Voudron didn't get into the car with them.

'Aren't you coming with us?' asked Biggles, genuinely surprised.

'No. You don't need me. My friend will take care of you.' Voudron shut the door.

The man got back into his seat. He touched a button and automatic blinds covered the windows. The car shot forward.

It was, as Ginger was of course aware, only a short distance to the Villa Mimosa, certainly not more than three minutes' drive from the mosque at the rate they were going. Wherefore as the minutes passed and the car showed no sign of stopping he began to get anxious. Had he been mistaken about their destination? But when, twenty minutes later, the car came to a stop, and they got out, he saw that he need not have worried. In the moonlight he recognized the entrance porch of the Villa Mimosa. Then he understood. The driver, unaware that they had seen the place before, had wasted time and petrol playing the old trick of trying to mislead them into thinking they had travelled about twenty miles instead of one. Raban was obviously taking no unnecessary chances.

The front door opened. A white-clad Arab invited them to enter. The car crept away to its garage.

Raban received them in a spacious library, and Ginger knew that from that moment there could be no turning back. The lawyer could not afford to let them go after seeing him and his establishment, for should they talk the French authorities would soon be on his track. Already he had committed himself to helping two potential deserters from the Legion. That was what it amounted to.

Raban invited them to be seated and opened the conversation in a manner so smoothly worded that he had obviously been through the procedure before.

'I hear you boys have had the bad luck to be posted to Fort Labougant,' he began, offering a box of cigars.

Biggles agreed this was so.

'You're English, eh?'

'*Oui, monsieur.*'

'Served in the Air Force.'

'*Oui, monsieur.*'

Raban shook his head sadly. 'That's what I say about these military men of ours. They get hold of a couple of useful chaps like you and the best thing they can think to do with you is put you where you would be absolutely wasted. It's a shame to send men such as you to the most God-forsaken place on earth. That's what I feel, and that's why I'm doing what I am. Sergeant Voudron, who I have met once or twice, happened to mention the matter to me the other evening when I ran into him. Of course, I shouldn't really be doing this, as I need hardly tell you. If it were known I should get into serious trouble—very serious indeed; for which reason I must ask for your solemn promise never to repeat this conversation to anyone. Of course, you yourselves, as deserters from the Legion, would be in a nasty position.'

Biggles and Ginger gave their assurance.

'Your names, I understand, are Biggs and Hepple?'

Biggles answered for both of them. 'Yes.'

'And you're both experienced pilots, able to fly at any time?'

'Yes.'

'In that case all you need is an aeroplane to put yourselves far beyond the reach of the French police.'

'But where can we find an aeroplane, monsieur?'

Raban waved his cigar. 'Don't worry about that. The question is, rather, what are you going to do after you have left North Africa? That is where I may be able to help you. Oh yes, I'll admit frankly that I have a personal interest in this matter. You see, I happen to

65

have a financial stake in an air-line operating company, and we are always on the look-out for good pilots. When I say good I mean pilots who are willing to undertake operations that might strike them as— well, shall we say unusual, and even useless. Why we do these things is our affair. All we ask is that the work is done without a lot of questions which, in the circumstances, might be justified. We pay our men well, of course.'

'Let us speak plainly, *monsieur*. You pay not only for pilotage but for silence.'

'Exactly.'

'And what sort of pay should we get, *monsieur*?'

'A hundred thousand francs a month, in any currency you like, with full board, lodging and expenses. Are you interested?'

'Interested!' Biggles smiled. 'After our beggarly few francs in the Legion?'

'You will each have a hundred thousand francs in your pocket when you leave here tonight.'

'A thousand thanks, *monsieur*.'

'You will not be sorry you have joined us,' declared Raban. 'We take care of those who serve us well. We have influential friends in high places who can be relied on to see that they come to no harm.'

'Would you permit me to ask a blunt question, *monsieur*?'

'You have every right to any question you like. We don't expect men to take a leap in the dark.'

'These operations of ours. Are they within the law?'

Raban looked shocked. 'Certainly they are. We are not criminals. I will be quite frank with you. The company for which we do a lot of work owns vast estates in several parts of the world—undeveloped parts of the world, I should explain. In such places there are sometimes to be found recalcitrant tribes-men who, by raiding our outposts, do a lot of mischief. To punish these rascals by chasing them on foot used to be a long and costly business. We find that aero-planes do the necessary chastisement faster and more efficiently. Naturally, we try to keep this quiet to pre-vent us from being bothered by well-meaning people who have nothing better to do than interfere with other people's business. But that is why we mostly use aircraft of military rather than civil types.'

'I understand,' murmured Biggles. 'As far as I am concerned the only question that remains to be asked, is when do we start.'

'Tonight, of course. There is no point in your going back to the barracks.'

That Biggles was not prepared for such a suggestion was apparent from his expression. Raban must have known this would come as a surprise to them, for he smiled. 'You see, we do not let grass grow under our feet.'

'But what about our personal kit?' demanded Biggles, not attempting to hide his disinclination to accept such arbitrary orders.

Raban made a gesture that brushed the objection aside. 'What personal kit of value could a legionnaire have? Surely there is nothing that we cannot replace—with something better, I hope. The toilet equipment issued by the French army is not of the best quality.'

This, of course, was true. They had nothing of value. But obviously Biggles didn't want to be cut off without a final word with Marcel. It was equally obvi-ous to Ginger that Raban had no intention of letting them out of his sight now he had revealed his treach-ery. He consoled himself with the thought that once in the air they would be able to go where they liked.

He took it for granted that they would have charge of the aircraft. But this cheerful thought was soon knocked on the head.

'What about clothes?' asked Biggles. 'Do we travel in these uniforms?'

Raban shrugged. 'Why not? No one will see you before you arrive at your destination.'

'But if we had to land somewhere we should be recognized as deserters!'

'That should discourage any temptation to land,' retorted Raban smoothly, with an implication that was not lost on Ginger. 'Let me assure you, you have nothing to worry about,' he went on. 'Everything is arranged.'

'Where is the place?'

'You'll see it in due course.'

'And what time do we leave here.'

'That, too, you will learn when the time comes.' Raban pulled open a drawer of his desk, and taking out two wads of notes, gave them one each. 'There is your first month's pay, with a bonus. Work out how long it would take you to earn as much money in the Legion. It should settle any doubts you may still entertain.'

'What about the course to our destination,' asked Biggles, showing that he, too, supposed they would be flying the aircraft. 'I would like to check it with the map.'

'You won't need anything like that,' returned Raban.

'Why not?'

'Your pilot will know where to go.'

'Our pilot?' Again Biggles stared.

'Of course. Had you supposed that you would be flying yourselves?'

'Yes,' replied Biggles frankly.

Raban shook his head. 'That would be too dangerous. You might lose your way. After all, as yet we have no proof of your ability.

'I see,' said Biggles.

'You will have to meet your pilot so it may as well be now,' stated Raban. 'You will have a meal together before you go.' He pressed the bell.

An Arab servant answered.

'Ask Monsieur Voss to come in,' ordered Raban.

This was another shock for Ginger. Voss! The deserter. The man who had bombed the Abyssinian village. So this is where he was, still working for the gang. Ginger looked at Biggles, but Biggles gave no sign that the name meant anything to him.

Voss came in. He was a slim, fair man in the middle twenties, good-looking in a hard sort of way. He had the typical square, close-cropped head of a Prussian. However, his manner, as he nodded to them, was cordial enough. 'Now we are going to fight on the same side, Englanders. That is as it should be,' he said, thus revealing that he had been informed of their recruitment. 'Have you finished with them, *monsieur*?' he asked Raban.

'Yes, they're all ready,' was the answer. 'I'll leave them in your hands. Give them a drink and see that they have a meal.'

'Certainly, *monsieur.*' Voss beckoned the two recruits. 'This way, comrades.'

Biggles and Ginger followed him to a small lounge, where they accepted a long iced drink, of which, it may be said, Ginger was badly in need. The rate at which things had gone had left him slightly dazed. Never had he been more anxious to discuss a situation with Biggles, and never had it been less possible.

Later, an Arab servant announced that dinner was served, so they went through to a small room next to the kitchen, where such a meal was served that had Ginger's appetite been normal he would have eaten more than he did. As it was, there was too much going on in his head to leave room for an appreciation of food. Raban did not appear. He was, presumably, eating alone in the dining-room in which they had seen him talking to Voudron.

'You'll find your new employers do you very well,' said Voss. 'Serve them well and they'll take care of you. Money is no object.'

He talked quite a lot, but was, Ginger noticed, careful not to give them any information. Biggles put in one or two prompting questions, but Voss switched the conversation every time. For the most part he talked 'shop', as if trying to check up on their air experience. There was obviously no haste about their departure.

It was after midnight when Voss got up, and after a glance at his watch announced casually that it was time they were on their way.

They went to the front door. The car was there, with the same black driver. They got in. The door slammed. The windows were shuttered. The car moved forward. There was nothing dramatic about it. Indeed, it was all as inconsequential as if they were going to a cinema. Certainly it was nothing like the scene Ginger had imagined. The fact that they were doing what they had set out to do, and it had all been made so easy, did nothing to restore his peace of mind. He had imagined that when they went both Marcel and the Air-Commodore would know about it. They might even know where they were going. Instead of which, he and Biggles were about to vanish as

70

completely as a stone dropped in an ocean. Nor was this accidental. He realized that from the moment they had met Voudron by the mosque they had been given no chance to speak to each other alone—much less speak to anyone else, or write a letter.

After a run of about twenty minutes the car stopped. Voss, saying they had arrived, got out. They would have a little way to walk. The car turned, and glided away.

Ginger, gazing about him, perceived they were on the edge of an aerodrome, lying white and silent in the moonlight, and a matter of perhaps half a mile from the hangars. Towards these, keeping on the road, Voss led the way.

After they had gone a hundred yards a notice-board appeared, clear and stark against the sky. As Ginger read it, and knew instantly what they were about to do, he felt his pulses tingle. For not only was this a military aerodrome of the French *Armée de l'Air*, but the home of Escadrille 77, from which at least one aircraft had already been stolen. Voss was now going to take another. As if this were not enough to daunt him he recalled what Marcel had said about extra guards being put on. Suppose they were caught in the act—with Voss, of all people? Given time, Marcel and the Air-Commodore would no doubt get them out of the mess: but long before that could happen they were likely to be shot out of hand, for the French must have had quite enough of Voss.

Did Voss know about the extra guards? Presumably not. And the dickens of it was they couldn't warn him without revealing how they knew, and this would betray them for what they were. Biggles was no doubt wrestling with the same problem. He said nothing, so

71

Ginger, too, remained silent, walking along behind Voss with his heart in his mouth, as the saying is.

What astonished Ginger was Voss's confidence. He behaved as though he knew a machine was there, waiting for them on the tarmac. If so, then obviously he had a confederate on the station.

At last Biggles spoke. He touched Voss on the arm. 'One moment, my friend,' he said softly. 'You will pardon us if we ask just what we are doing. Is it the intention to—er—borrow a French Air Force machine.'

'Exactly. But don't let it worry you. One will be waiting for us.'

'But I understand we are going a long way. What about petrol.'

'The tanks will be full. Didn't I say everything would be ready? Don't ask fool questions. Wait here while I make sure everything is in order. I shall be five minutes at most.'

'*Bon**.'

Voss went on towards the hangars, at last giving Ginger a chance to say what was on his mind.

'We're crazy,' he told Biggles grimly. 'You remember what Marcel said about extra guards.'

'Yes. We shall have to chance it. The guards may have been bribed for all we know. Anyway, I'm not going to turn back now. This is what we came for.'

'All right. And suppose we get away with it, what are we going to do? Bomb innocent people? Not likely. Yet if we refuse, or fail, we shall certainly be bumped off.'

'We shall know definitely that the secret air force exists, where it is stationed, and its purpose. There's

* French: Good.

bound to be a connecting link between the squadron and those who control it. We'll watch for it.'

'There must also be a connecting link between Raban and the same people. We could watch him without putting our necks in a noose.'

'Maybe. But we stand a better chance by working inside the racket than watching it from the outside. That's enough. Here comes Voss.'

The German returned. 'All clear,' he announced. 'The machine's ready. Tanks full. A touch will start her. We'll be in the air before these useless mechanics wake up.'

'I hope you're right,' said Ginger softly.

'No noise now,' whispered Voss, and led the way.

Ginger soon saw that he had told the truth.

On the concrete apron that fronted the gaping doors of a hangar stood an aircraft of the light-bomber type bearing the blue, white and red roundel of the French Air Force. As they walked quietly towards it a man wearing the badges of rank of a corporal appeared out of the shadows. He whispered something to Voss.

So this, thought Ginger, was the traitor. He hoped one day to have the pleasure of denouncing him. Indeed, it needed all his self-control not to do so there and then. He looked around with trepidation. Where were the guards of which Marcel had spoken? Were they all asleep? There was not a soul in sight. A feeling came over him that the place was too quiet; that the uncanny silence was itself a threat. He tried to shake off the sensation, but it persisted, and he wished himself anywhere but where he was. 'If we're going, for heaven's sake let's go,' he muttered.

Voss gave him a disdainful glance, as if contemptuous of his fears, and walked over to the aircraft, which was, of course, in complete darkness, showing no navigation lights.

They got in. Voss took Biggles into the cockpit with him. Ginger, in the navigator's compartment just behind, looked out of a side window to see the corporal waving them off. The twin engines whirred and started. Instantly, as if it had been a signal, the tarmac came to life. A whistle shrilled. A man shouted an order. Dark figures, running, converged on the aircraft. The engines bellowed. The machine began to move. The corporal ran. A pistol spat. He fell, writhing. There were more shots. Some hit the machine, now gaining speed. Ginger flung himself flat as bullets smacked through the fuselage. The only thought in his racing brain was, so the guards were on the job after all.

The windows became squares of white light as a searchlight caught the aircraft in its beam and held it. A machine-gun opened up, and Ginger flinched as lead lashed the machine like a flail. Splinters flew. He bunched himself into a ball, thinking the undercarriage must be wiped off, as the aircraft swerved sickeningly. This was the end, he thought. Why didn't Voss switch off, the fool. A crash now and they would be in flames.

He breathed again as the Breguet became airborne. A reek of petrol in his nostrils told its own story. Dimly, as in a delirium, he heard Biggles shouting.

Getting up he staggered forward.

Chapter 7
Death in the Air

For the next ten minutes all Ginger's worst nightmares seemed to be happening together. He could hear Biggles calling but to get to him, anxious though he was to obey, was another matter. For one thing he was in darkness and the lay-out of the aircraft unfamiliar. But what put him in a state near to panic was the way the machine was behaving. It was all over the sky, and clearly, if not out of control, nearly so. As it swung about, centrifugal force jammed him first against one side, then the other. On top of this he was half choked by petrol fumes, and expected the machine to go up in flames at any moment.

At first, as he clawed his way through the bulkhead door, he thought Biggles must have been hit. Then he thought it was the machine that had been damaged, having had its controls shot away. But it turned out to be neither of these things. One look was enough to explain everything.

It was Voss who had been hit. He was either dead or unconscious. Not having had time to strap himself in his limp body had fallen and jammed itself against the control column. From the second pilot's seat Biggles was trying to hold him up with one hand while he endeavoured to keep the aircraft on even keel with the other. In this he was only partly successful, and the behaviour of the machine was accounted for. Ginger rushed to help him.

'Get him out of that seat,' panted Biggles. 'Get

him into the cabin—out of my way—anywhere. We shall hit something in a minute if I don't get that stick back.'

Between them, with the Breguet still yawing, side-slipping and nearly stalling, they got the unconscious German into his seat, and then, with a great effort, behind it. This enabled Biggles to steady the machine, with the result that Ginger had no great difficulty in dragging the limp body into the cabin, where, gasping for breath, he nearly collapsed on top of him. What to do next he didn't know. He was finding it hard to think at all. He couldn't have done much for the wounded man had it been daylight. In the dark he could do nothing. The stench of petrol was such that there could be no question of striking a match.

He staggered back to Biggles. 'What are you going to do?'

'Get my bearings.'

'Well for heaven's sake try to get it down.'

'For several reasons I'm not going back to the aero-drome, even if I could find it.'

'You'd better find somewhere quickly. Voss is about all in and the cabin's swimming with petrol.'

'The gravity tank was hit. The others are still show-ing pressure. Don't get in a flap. This needs thinking about.'

'I can't see that it needs any thinking about,' declared Ginger. 'I'm all for getting down.'

'If we land near that airfield after what we've done we shall be for the high jump.'

'If we could get down close enough to barracks to get there before daylight who's to know we had any-thing to do with pinching the machine?'

'That crooked corporal may squeal.'

'Squeal nothing. He was shot. I saw him fall. What about Voss, anyway. We ought to give him a chance.'

'Is he alive?'

'I don't know.'

'Try to find out. I think he was hit through the neck.'

Ginger went back to the cabin. He was just in time to hear the death rattle in Voss's throat. He returned to Biggles. 'He's had it,' he announced.

Biggles was silent for a moment. Then he said: 'Bad luck. Still he's been asking for it for a long time. I wonder we didn't all get it. As there's nothing we can do for him I feel inclined to go on. The machine seems to be holding together. Go through Voss's pockets and see if you can find a map, a compass course, anything that might tell us where he was making for. Bring the stuff here, where you can see it in the light of the instrument panel.'

Ginger returned to the cabin, emptied the dead man's pockets and took the contents to the cockpit, where he went through them.

'Well?' asked Biggles.

'Nothing. He knew where he was going so he had no need to put it in writing.'

'That settles any argument about trying to get to the place; and since we have to go down it might as well be as soon as we can find a flat patch.'

'Well buck up about it,' pleaded Ginger. 'If these petrol fumes reach one of the exhausts—'

'All right—all right,' rapped out Biggles. 'I know. Don't make a song about it.'

'Look at the searchlights,' muttered Ginger. 'We don't need two guesses at what they're looking for. After what has happened every police and military

77

station in North Africa must be on the watch for us. If radar picks us up—'

He crouched as the staccato chatter of multiple machine-guns came over the drone of the motors. Several bullets hit the machine. 'That's a fighter—' He got no farther, for the machine went into an almost vertical sideslip, pressing him into his seat. Whether it was intentional or not he did not know, but he thought it was the end.

The machine came out of the slip, turned twice in a vertical bank and returned to even keel. 'Try to pick out a spot that will give us a chance to get on the carpet,' said Biggles calmly. 'We can't shoot back.'

Ginger stared down. The first thing he saw was a fighter flashing through a searchlight beam. Below, the ground was a vague shadow, half hidden under what he took be to heat haze. Farther away, to the south, he could see moonlight glistening on what looked like sand; but whether it was level or broken by dunes it was impossible to tell.

'Swing to the right and go a bit lower,' he said hoarsely, for his throat was dry with strain.

Biggles obliged. The engines died. Losing height, the aircraft droned on through the moonlit night under a sky ablaze with stars.

After that Biggles took matters into his own hands. He didn't speak, so Ginger was unaware that he intended to try a landing until he saw palm fronds almost brushing the fuselage. Then came a violent jar as the wheels touched. The machine bounced high. The engines did not open up again, so Ginger, knowing what was coming, put his hands over his head and lifted his knees to his chin in the hope of saving them from being broken.

He had not long to wait. The machine sank like a

wounded bird. There was a crash like the end of the world. Sand flew in all directions. Then, suddenly, silence, an unreal hush broken by the drip of petrol spilling from fractured leads.

Ginger needed no invitation to get out, for no man moves faster than a pilot removing himself from a petrol-soaked aircraft knowing that one spark from a dying magneto* is all that is necessary to explode the airframe as if it were a bomb. The fact that Biggles had switched off, as he knew he would have done, did not entirely ensure safety.

Ginger fought his way out of the mess like a madman. He took one swift look to make sure Biggles was following, then he ran—or rather, stumbled, for his feet sank into soft, yielding sand. Not until he had put thirty yards between him and the wreck did he stop, and then he sank to the ground, breathless and weak from shock.

Biggles joined him. 'We're well out of that,' he observed without emotion.

'That's—what comes—of associating—with a crook like Voss,' contended Ginger cuttingly.

'At least we haven't come out of it as badly as he has,' Biggles pointed out. 'The gang has lost a good pilot.'

'I felt in my bones all along that he wasn't going to get away with another machine as easily as that. The French aren't fools. We should have warned him—'

'Just a minute,' interposed Biggles. 'Suppose we forget the past and deal with the present? That should keep us occupied for some time.'

---

* A generator using permanent magnets to produce an electric current, in this case for the ignition of the petrol mixture in the engine.

'Okay. What are you going to do next?' Feeling somewhat recovered Ginger got up.

'I'm going to try to get back to camp. There's nothing else we can do.'

'About how far are we away?'

'Fifteen to twenty miles as near as I can guess. As you may have noticed, we didn't exactly fly a straight course.'

'I noticed it all right,' murmured Ginger. 'Do you happen to know where we are?'

'I've no idea beyond a general impression that we're somewhere south-west of the camp. I hadn't much time for looking at the ground but it looked like a sparsely-populated district, fringing desert country. What I took to be a flat stretch of sand had some sand dunes running across it.'

'I noticed that, too,' murmured Ginger. 'Or at any rate, the one we hit.' He gazed towards the four points of the compass in turn. To the south, east and west, the terrain appeared to be much the same—typical rough, undulating ground, mostly sand, broken by occasional stands of date palms and flourishing growths of prickly pear. Only to the north, as was to be expected, did the country show signs of human occupation. But the moon was now low over the horizon, and in its deceptive light it was hard to see anything distinctly. Only the wrecked aircraft stood out hard and sharp against the sky. 'What are you going to do about Voss?' he asked.

'Leave him where he is. That suits our book—not that there's anything else we can do. When it gets light, and people start moving about, someone will spot the crash. As Voss is known to the authorities it will be assumed that he took the machine. The bullet holes will speak for themselves. It will also be assumed,

I hope, that Voss was alone. If the Corporal was killed he won't be able to talk. Voss can't talk either. The only other man in the know is Raban, and he's not likely to talk. Our plan, obviously, is to get back to camp as quickly as we can—or at all events, remove ourselves as far as possible from the machine so that we shan't be associated with it. If you've got your breath back let's start walking.'

'What's Voudron going to say when he sees us?'

'I don't care what he says. We'll tell him the truth about what happened at the airfield.'

'If we could find a telephone, or somehow get in touch with Raban, he'd send his car for us, and perhaps hide us until he can make other arrangements for us. Otherwise, for being absent without leave, even if we're not charged with attempted desertion, we look like spending the next few weeks in cells.'

'You seem to have overlooked one good reason why we can't contact Raban,' Biggles pointed out. 'We're not supposed to know where he lives. He took precautions to prevent us from knowing that. To ring him up, or to turn up at the villa, would create a situation I prefer not to face. We'll let him get in touch with us, as he will, no doubt, if we can get back to camp. The difficulty will be to do that without being seen. These uniforms are conspicuous. Everyone knows them. Just a minute while I put Voss's things back in his pockets.'

A few minutes later, turning their faces to the north, they started walking.

To Ginger, this was a weary business. All they saw for the first hour was an Arab encampment, one of those of a semi-permanent character. Making a detour round it they came upon a second-class road. This they followed for another hour without seeing anyone though they were now in more cultivated country, the crops being mostly the lupins used for fodder. Then a vineyard, and some fields of the scented geranium grown for the perfume trade, warned them that they were now in the region of white colonists. By this time the eastern sky was aglow with the dawn of another day.

Then, suddenly, they came upon a house. Set in trees, they did not see it until they were level with the front entrance. There a man was loading a decrepid *camionette** with vegetables for market. He saw them before they could take steps to prevent it. Ginger, who was deadly tired, didn't care particularly.

The cultivator greeted them in French with the cheerful verbosity of his kind. Of course, he wanted to know what they were doing there, and where they were going. Biggles told him they were on their way back to camp at Zebrit after a wild night at the end of which they had lost their way—all of which was perfectly true.

'You must have drunk a lot of wine,' declared the farmer, laughing. 'You're fifteen miles from home.'

Biggles did not deny the implied charged of being drunk. 'Where are we now?' he asked.

'You're five miles from Chella. That's the nearest village.'

Ginger's heart went into his boots.

'Is there a telephone there?' asked Biggles.

The farmer said there was. There was also a light railway. He was going there presently, to put his produce on the line for Oran. Would they like a lift?'

Biggles said they would, very much. He explained that they were anxious to get back to camp before

* French: van.

the police started looking for two deserters. This was so feasible that the man accepted the explanation without question.

So, presently, to Ginger's great relief, they were on their way, bumping and rattling over the rough road. He didn't mind how bumpy the road was. Anything was better than trudging through the heat of the day. A half-ripe pomegranate, plucked from an overhanging tree, gave him some refreshment, and he looked at the landscape with less critical eyes. Things might have been worse, he soliloquized. Much worse.

The trouble occurred in Chella. Biggles would have preferred to dismount outside the village and approach in a manner less conspicuous; but he couldn't very well say that to the good-natured driver who, after pointing out the road to Zebrit, put them down outside the little post-office. Biggles did actually intend to ring up the camp to explain their absence, for there was no longer any hope of getting back unobserved. In any case they would have been missed at roll-call.

This plan was frustrated by the arrival on the scene of the local gendarme. He came strolling round the corner; but when he saw the legionnaires he moved with alacrity. This attracted the attention of the passers-by and in a moment the place was buzzing with excitement.

The policeman, who had obviously been informed that two legionnaires were missing, wanted to arrest them. The farmer told him not to be a fool. The men were already on their way back to camp. They had told him so. Hadn't he given them a lift? The policeman objected. The spectators, as so often happens in France, took the side of the victims of the law. The babble rose to such a pitch that Ginger gave up trying to follow the argument. He sat on the running-board. It broke under his weight and he fell in the dust. This was the sort of humour the people understood and they roared with laughter. A man produced a bottle of wine; another, a packet of cigarettes. Ginger, who wasn't in the mood to be funny, grinned sheepishly. Even the gendarme smiled. Seeing that he was in the minority he took a less officious view. He agreed with the cultivator (who seemed to have a fixed idea that the two soldiers had been drunk overnight) that he himself had, on occasion, taken more wine than was good for him.

Biggles then put in a word. '*Monsieur,*' said he, addressing the gendarme, 'I will do whatever you say. I admit that last night my comrade and myself were slightly *fou* (tipsy). But what's wrong with that?'

'Nothing,' shouted the crowd.

'After all, where would you sell your wine if nobody drunk it?'

'Quite right,' chanted the crowd. 'Bravo for the good soldiers.'

'Now, *monsieur,* we are in your hands,' went on Biggles, still speaking to the gendarme. 'We shall not attempt to run away. It was my intention, as our friend here will confirm, to ring up the camp. That is why he brought us here. Now we will do it, or you may do it, as you wish.'

'I will do it.'

'*Bon.* We will wait.'

The gendarme went into the post-office, from which he emerged presently to say that an escort was on the way to take them back to camp. Meantime, while they were waiting, would they care for a cup of coffee and a *croissant*?

Biggles accepted the invitation, so chairs were put

on the pavement outside the café and very soon they were all friends together. Satisfied, for this was the way such affairs should end, the crowd began to disperse. It suited Ginger, too.

When, half an hour later, a service truck pulled up, who was in charge of the escort but Voudron. In his official capacity he was able to take the prisoners a little to one side. 'What happened?' he asked anxiously.

'Guards were on watch,' answered Biggles. 'They opened fire on us. We got the machine but they shot us down.'

'What about the corporal?'

'He was shot—killed I think.'

'And Voss?'

'Dead.'

'Where's the body?'

'We left it in the machine—ten or twelve miles from here. What else could we do?'

'Nothing. Did anyone see you near the crash?'

'No.'

'Good. Don't worry. You'll be all right. Come on.'

Voudron strode to the trunk, followed by his willing prisoners.

Chapter 8
A Ring Tells a Tale

On arrival at the barracks Biggles and Ginger were put on a charge, as they knew they would be, for not being in their quarters at 'lights out.' This was not a serious offence, for it was a common occurrence, so the officer before whom they were taken was their own company commander, Marcel. This, as Ginger looked at it, had its humorous aspect. But there was nothing comical about the proceedings.

Marcel had, of course, done the regular two years compulsory military service, and knew the rules. With a face as grave as a judge he listened to their explanation of how they had lost their way (knowing perfectly well that it was complete fabrication) and then gave them a dressing down in the sternest army tradition. He concluded by sentencing them both to ten days' Confined to Barracks. This was the usual punishment for such a breach of discipline, and they realized that however reluctant he may have been to do this, knowing how it would hamper their movements, with Voudron present he could not do otherwise. The sergeant was not a fool, and anything that looked like leniency might have give him food for thought. They were at least free within the precincts of the camp, so it might have been worse.

Nothing was said in the orderly-room about the affair at the aerodrome, but, as they presently discovered, the camp was buzzing with the news, which was now public property. There was no reason whatsoever why they should be associated with it. Voudron knew the truth, of course. Marcel might guess it, and be anxious to question them; but here again their respective ranks made this impossible until a method of communication could be devised. However, later in the day Marcel managed to pass near them on the square. Without checking his stride he said as they saluted: 'Where you in that plane?' Biggles answered 'Yes.' There was no time for more, but it was enough to let them know that Marcel had summed up the situation correctly.

Voudron was soon after them for further particulars. Biggles told him the truth. There was no need to prevaricate. As he said at the finish, there was nothing they could do about it, and they were lucky to be alive. Had he, Biggles, been in the pilot's seat, he could have 'had it' instead of Voss, whose misfortune it was to be on the side nearest the gunners. 'What happens next?' he asked.

'You'll get your orders in due course, no doubt,' Voudron told him.

'Does your friend want his money back?'

'Certainly not. Once you're on his pay-roll you stay on it—until . . .'

'Until what?'

'Until you've no further use for money,' answered Voudron with an unpleasant grin, and strode away.

In view of their confinement to barracks Biggles did not expect any developments until the period of punishment expired. They themselves were helpless, but Marcel, they thought, might find a way to speak to them; but far from this happening they did not even see him. This surprised them, and as the days passed they discussed the mystery more often. Ginger was confident that Marcel, knowing that his usefulness

87

at the camp had ended as a result of his conversation with Joudrier, had taken Biggles's advice and gone back to Paris. They might expect a letter any post. But Biggles could not believe that he had departed without a word, and was worried. Still, there was nothing they could do. They were in no position to ask questions.

They did not think Raban would be able to move, either, a belief supported by the way Voudron kept clear of them. But Biggles saw another reason for this. The rumour about the draft going to Labougant had fizzled out, and Voudron might have found it difficult to explain his lies. However, on the fifth day of their confinement, in the middle of all this conjecture, Voudron indicated by an inclination of his head that he wanted to speak to them, so they followed him to the place where they had conspired on the previous occasion.

He came straight to the point. 'Do you know the way out of camp over the wall behind the kitchens? There are two loose bricks.'

'Of course,' answered Biggles. Everyone knew this exit, which was supposed to be a secret. It had been used for so long, according to report, that Biggles was sure the officers knew about it, but turned a blind eye.

'Good,' said Voudron. 'Go over the wall tonight at twelve midnight exactly.'

Biggles's eyebrows went up. 'You mean—break camp?'

'Certainly. Somebody wants to see you. A car will be there to pick you up. There's no risk. You won't be away long.'

'Will you be there?'

'No. That's all. Those were my instructions.'

'We'll be there,' promised Biggles.

Voudron went off.

'Here we go again,' murmured Ginger, as they strolled back to their quarters. 'Are you going on with it?'

'Of course. But this losing touch with Marcel is a nuisance. I'd like him to know what we're doing.'

They spent the rest of the day watching for him, but without success. Ginger did not say so, but an uneasy feeling was growing on him that Marcel had fallen foul of the Arabs whose first attempt to kill him had failed.

Twelve midnight found them at the wall behind the kitchens. They had never used the place, but they had heard about it from others, and they had no difficulty in finding the two loose bricks that enabled the barrier to be scaled. There was no one in sight, but no sooner had they dropped to the far side than the promised car moved towards them from the shadows in which it had been waiting.

Thereafter the procedure was as before. The windows were covered, and after a drive of about twenty minutes they found themselves at the Villa Mimosa. They were taken straight in to Raban. He was not alone. In an easy chair, placed just outside the radius of light and half turned away, sat an elderly man, smoking a cigar. All Ginger could really see of him was a beard, a bald head, and dark glasses.

Raban's manner was crisp but not discourteous. He invited them to be seated, offered cigarettes, and then said: 'I have brought you here so that I can hear from your own lips exactly what happened the other night.'

Ginger noted that he did not introduce the stranger, or even refer to him.

Biggles answered. 'Voudron will have given you the main facts, *monsieur*, as I gave them to him when he

89

came to fetch us.' He then went on to describe, step by step, the events that had cost Voss his life.

'What was your impression of this unfortunate business?' asked Raban. 'Did it strike you that there might have been treachery somewhere?'

'No, I wouldn't say that,' replied Biggles slowly. 'I simply thought that the guards which had been posted—as they would be, of course—were singularly alert. We didn't make a sound. Voss wasn't expecting anything to happen. Nor was the corporal we met. We were just taking off when the guards rushed us. The only thing that struck me as odd was, they didn't challenge us. They opened fire straightaway. But, of course, as the engines were running they may have thought that was the only way of stopping us. Voss was hit just as the machine was leaving the ground. Not having had time to strap himself in he fell against the control column and I had some difficulty in keeping the machine under control. After we were in the air we found that Voss was dead. The machine had been badly shot about and fighters were still shooting at us, so I decided to land. Had I known where we were bound for I would have tried to carry on. As a matter of fact we searched Voss to see if he had a map on him, or any other indication of his objective. We left him in the crash just as it was and then decided to make back for camp, having nowhere else to go. Had we known where to find you we would have got in touch with you to let you know what had happened.'

Raban was silent for a moment. 'There is no suspicion in the camp that you were concerned with the affair?'

'None whatever—as far as we know.'

'The object of these questions,' explained Raban,

'is to ascertain why the plan miscarried. We feel there must have been a leak or the guards would not have been on the spot, and so wide-awake.'

Biggles shook his head. 'I'm afraid I can't help you there, *monsieur*. We didn't know where we were going, or what was going to happen, until we got to the aerodrome.'

'Oh, I'm not blaming you,' answered Raban quickly. 'On the contrary, in the circumstances you did very well. But now let us deal with the future. The death of Voss has left us in urgent need of a pilot. This, obviously, is not the moment to try to repeat our last experiment in this region, so it is my intention to send you away from here by a more regular method. Do you know Alexandria?'

'I have been there, *monsieur*, but I can't say I know it very well.'

'It isn't really important. You will be able to find your way. Tomorrow night you will leave the camp as you did tonight, at the same hour. You will be brought here, where you will be given final instructions and provided with civilian clothes and other things you will need. My car will take you to an airport some distance from here and you'll be on your way East before you're missed from camp. This time there will be no mistake. You'll be able to shake the dust of the barrack square from your boots for ever. That's all for now. Be careful who you speak to and what you say. There are spies about. My car will take you back to camp.' Raban touched a bell.

Twenty minutes later, at the faulty wall behind the kitchens, Biggles and Ginger watched the car that had brought them back fade into the moonlight. Said Biggles: 'Well, that was a useful night's work. Now we know for certain what goes on. You saw the old man in the chair?'

'Yes.'

'You recognized him?'

'No.'

'Unless I'm losing my eyesight it was Johann Klutz, chief operator for the armaments king, the late Julius Rothenburg. His photograph was among those the Air Commodore dug out for us. It was a bad one admittedly, a copy of a passport photo taken years ago. He's aged a lot since then, and he took care to keep in the background; but I'm sure that's who it was. I told the chief that I thought he might still be in the same racket. I'm not saying he's the king-pin. He was Rothenburg's chief of staff, and probably holds the same position with his successors. That's why he's here now. He'd want to know at first hand how the plan to pinch that Breguet came unstuck. The value of the machine wouldn't upset him. It would be the fact that the French guards were on the job, as if they had been forewarned. And I'll tell you something else. A thought has just occurred to me, possibly because we're booked for the Middle East. A day or two ago there was a news item in the papers about tension on the Iraq-Persian* frontier flaring up again. It wouldn't surprise me if that's the work of the gang. It's right up their street. If so, it may explain why they're hurrying us along, to do one of their dirty jobs in that . . . what are you staring at?'

Ginger, who had been examining closely a small object that he held in the palm of his hand, looked up. 'Marcel's ring,' he answered in a strained voice.

'What do you mean?'

* Now Iranian-Iraqi border area.

92

'You remember that signet ring Marcel always wore on the little finger of his left hand?'

'Yes.'

'This is it.'

'Where did you find it?'

'In the car. When I got in my hand slipped behind the seat. There was something there. I could feel it was a ring, but I've only just had a chance to look at it.'

Biggles took the ring. 'You're right. That's Marcel's ring,' he confirmed, in a voice stiff with shock and sudden anxiety. 'He must have been in that car. It couldn't have got there any other way.'

'Which means they've killed him.'

'Not necessarily. Had they simply wanted to kill him they could have done so without putting him in the car. They've got him. We needn't doubt that. Whether the ring slipped off his finger in a struggle, or whether he deliberately pushed it off hoping we'd find it doesn't matter. He's been in that car. They're holding him—if nothing worse. We can't leave him in their hands, for if we do they'll certainly kill him when they're finished with him—if they haven't done so already. But I don't think he was dead when he was in that car.'

'Why would they want him alive?'

'They knew, through Voudron, that he was a police agent. They would, therefore, be very anxious indeed to know what he was doing here; and if he was on their track they would have to know how much he knew. If they killed him they'd learn nothing. Which is why I think they took him alive.'

'If they've got him, and he's still alive, he'll be in the Villa Mimosa.'

'I imagine so.'

'We can't leave him there.'

'Of course we can't. The problem is to know what to do about it, for it seems that whatever we do we shall queer our pitch for tomorrow night, and be left at a dead end just as we were getting somewhere. I could kick myself for not realizing the reason for Marcel's disappearance.'

'Pity Raban didn't give us the address of the place he's sending us to in Alexandria. We might have picked up the trail again from there.'

'He's too experienced a schemer to part with information before it's necessary. We still know no more than we did when we went out tonight. Believe you me, when we start tomorrow night we shall be watched until we are in the plane—and perhaps all the way to Alexandria. These crooks can't afford to take a million to one chance of anything going wrong, and they know it.'

'Very well. Then what do we do about Marcel? We can't leave things as they are.'

'I've no intention of doing so. I'm going back to the Villa. There's just a possibility that we may be able to locate Marcel. 'If we fail I shall contact Joudrier in Paris, tell him what we suspect, and leave the decision to him. If he raids the Villa, and that's all he can do, he cuts the trail, but I see no alternative. I only hope he's in time to save Marcel.'

'You haven't forgotten we're confined to barracks?'

'If it's necessary to contact Joudrier I shan't return to barracks.'

'What about the local police?'

'A fat lot of notice they'd take of two stray legionnaires. They might start making enquiries, and by that time Raban would know we'd been to the police. Come on. We'll keep off the road. To be spotted out

94

of camp, and thrown into cells at this stage, would just about put the lid on everything.'

They had no great distance to go and they made the best time possible. As was to be expected at such an hour of night they saw no one on the way. They found the Villa silent and in darkness. The white walls and the gardens were drenched in moonlight. The crickets had stopped chirping. The gate was locked.

'Over the wall,' whispered Biggles.

This was easily accomplished, and in a minute they were inside, crouching in the cage-like shadows of a group of bamboos.

Behind them, suddenly, a leaf rustled.

Biggles spun round.

'Okay, it's me,' breathed a voice. The speaker was Algy.

He joined them in the shadows.

'So you got my letter,' said Biggles.

'Yes. What are you doing here at this hour?'

'Marcel is missing. We believe he's here. I suppose you haven't seen anything of him.'

'No. The car has been out several times but you can never see who's in it.'

'How long have you been here?'

'Since yesterday evening. When I got your letter I went to the chief. As things were quiet he said I'd better come out here with Bertie to see if you needed help. We went to Paris to have a word with Captain Joudrier about the position and then came straight on here, dressed as casual tourists.'

'Pity you didn't bring Joudrier with you,' muttered Biggles.

'We did. Or rather, he came with us.'

'Good. Where is he?'

'In the town, staying at our hotel. We're taking it

in turns to watch this place. At the same time we watched the road, thinking we might see you.'

'At the moment we're doing ten days' C.B.,' explained Biggles drily. 'But never mind about that. Things are moving fast. We're booked tomorrow night for Alexandria. We were told that only a few minutes ago. Now we find Marcel's signet ring in Raban's car, which means they've got him—if nothing worse. We couldn't go, leaving him here, so we came back to see if we could do anything about it.'

'Then you were in the car that went out about half an hour ago.'

'Yes.'

'What are you going to do now?'

Biggles thought for a moment. 'If I knew the gang's headquarters in Alex. I'd ask Joudrier to raid this place tonight, to get Marcel out. But I don't. So if we do anything now we shall cut the trail.'

'I see that.'

'All right. I feel that if Marcel is alive he'll still be alive at this time tomorrow night, so we shall lose nothing by waiting twenty-four hours. We're to come back here tomorrow midnight for final orders, tickets and civvy clothes. We shall be taken by car to an official airfield, which is almost certain to be Algiers— Oran being a bit too close to Sidi bel Abbes—and then fly by regular service to Alex., as I understand it, without an escort. Tell Joudrier what I suggest is this. When Raban's car goes out any time after midnight we shall presumably be in it. Let it go, then raid the place and rescue Marcel. If it turns out that we're wrong, and Marcel isn't here, Joudrier will have to act as he thinks best. In any case, you and Bertie could make a dash for Algiers and perhaps get on the Alex. plane with us. Don't recognize us in case we're watched; but when we get out you could follow us to see where we go. Joudrier will grab Raban's car and the black driver when it comes back. If he can do all this without a word getting into the newspapers the rest of the gang won't know what's happened, and that'd give us a better chance. Tell him to hold Raban on some minor offence. Not a word about deserters from the Legion.'

'I get it,' murmured Algy.

'Here, briefly, is the gen for Joudrier. The recruiting agent for the gang in the camp is Sergeant Voudron. He's the go-between between the camp and this house, which is where the desertions are organized; which means that Raban is an important man. In the house at the moment is Johann Klutz, who used to work for Rothenburg, the armaments king. He only came here I think to hear our story of how the attempt to get away with a French Breguet failed the other night, so he may leave at any time. If so, you'll have to let him go.'

'Were you in that airfield affair?'

'In it? We were in the machine. But I've no time to tell you about that now. Voss was killed. That's left the gang short of a pilot, which is why, I believe, they're rushing us through. There's probably another one of these bombing jobs in the offing.'

'And you think they may detail you to do it.'

'I'm hoping that from Alexandria we shall be sent on to one of the gang's secret airfields.'

'And then what?'

'I don't know. It's no use trying to take our fences before we come to them. Have I made everything clear?'

'Quite.'

'Good. Then we'll get back to camp. You'd better

keep watch here until Bertie comes to relieve you. Then put all the cards in front of Joudrier. This is really his territory, not ours.'

'Fair enough. Are you going to have a look round while you're here?'

Biggles hesitated. 'No,' he decided. 'There's really no point in it now you're here. I'll leave that to you. Things are going well, and I'd rather not risk upsetting everything by being seen near here after being taken back to camp. It wouldn't matter so much if you were seen.'

Algy switched the subject. 'Have you read today's papers?'

'No. Why?'

'Your mention of Alexandria reminded me. On the list of men who might possibly be associated with the racket—I mean the list the Air-Commodore got out—was a Greek oil magnate named Nestor Janescu. He lived mostly aboard a luxury yacht at Cannes, on the Riviera.'

'I remember. What about him?'

'Only that the yacht, *Silvanus*, has arrived at Alex. As you look like going there I thought it worth mentioning.'

'Quite right. I'll bear it in mind. But we must be getting back to camp. Come on, Ginger.'

Leaving Algy watching the house they set off for the broken wall.

Chapter 9
Aladdin's Lamp

The following day passed without incident, and when the time arrived Biggles and Ginger went out over the wall. The car was there to pick them up, and after its usual tour to mislead them put them down at the front door of the Villa Mimosa. Everything appeared to be normal. There was, of course, no sign of Algy and the others, but Ginger knew they would not be far away.

Raban was waiting for them. He was alone, so whether Klutz had departed, or was still in the house, they did not know. Everything was ready, Raban assured them, and showed them to an ante-room where two complete sets of civilian clothes—the ordinary white linen suits generally worn south of the Mediterranean—had been laid out. They took off their uniforms for the last time and rejoined Raban, who handed them their air tickets for Alexandria. Glancing at his before putting it in his pocket Ginger saw that Biggles had been correct in the matter of the airport. It was Maison Blanche, Algiers.

Raban then gave them each what appeared to be a small club badge, in the shape of an oriental lamp with a number in the centre, to be worn in the button-hole. Ginger's number was 122, and Biggles's he noticed, was 123. This, said Raban, was the only sign of identification they would need when they reached their destination, where they would receive further instructions. It was then revealed that this was a nightclub named Aladdin's Lamp, in the Stretta Albani, which was in the dock quarter. All they had to do was go there and sit down. They were expected, so thereafter there would be no need for them to do anything but obey orders. If they were ready they could start immediately, as they had some way to go.

'Do we sleep at this club, or at an hotel?' asked Biggles. 'The question arises as to whether we find accommodation and then go to the club, or—'

'You will go to an hotel,' interposed Raban. 'That is arranged.'

'Very well, *monsieur*. We're ready.'

Raban saw them to the door. The car was waiting. They got in. The car moved off.

All this was as Biggles had visualized it, and had discussed it with Ginger at some length. The main point of their debate had been whether or not to let the man drive them to the airport. Knowing where they were going, with identification badges in their buttonholes and tickets in their pockets, the driver was of no further use to them. He would be arrested on his return, anyway. There was, therefore, nothing to prevent them from seizing him there and then, and waiting while the villa was raided. Biggles had been greatly tempted to adopt this plan, for there were many advantages to be gained by it. They would be able to speak to Joudrier, and learn if Marcel was in the house. They would also be able to give Algy their address in Alexandria, for should he miss the plane, or find seats booked to capacity, he would lose touch with them. Alexandria was a big place and they were not likely to be there long.

But in the end Biggles decided not to risk it, for one reason only. The man might have had instructions to hand them over to someone at the airport. If, therefore, they arrived without him, the person waiting would know something was amiss, with consequences fatal to their investigations, if not their lives. How well advised Biggles was in this decision they were soon to learn.

It was a long run to Algiers, but the plane did not leave until six and they arrived with half an hour to spare. Going through to the waiting-room (accompanied by their driver, Ginger noticed) the first person they saw was the bearded man they had seen in the Villa Mimosa, the man whom Biggles had thought was Klutz. Although he still wore dark glasses, in broad daylight there was no longer any doubt about it. Biggles would have taken no notice of him had he not given them a nod of recognition.

'Haven't we met before,' he enquired.

'Possibly,' answered Biggles cautiously. 'When I was a small boy I was taught when travelling never to speak to strangers.'

'Quite right. But you needn't be afraid to speak to me, now, if you want to.'

How this conversation would have ended is a matter for speculation, but at this juncture there occurred an incident that clearly made Klutz indisposed to pursue it.

It was apparently to confirm this meeting that the driver had followed them in, for now, with a grin, he went out. They never saw him again. At the same time a man arrived with a load of newspapers and began to open his kiosk. Klutz went over, bought a paper, returned to his seat and opened it. As his eyes fell on the printed page his face turned ashen, and for a moment he was so agitated that he dropped his glasses. Ginger hurried to pick them up. 'Are you ill, sir?' he asked quickly.

'No—no. Take no notice.' With an obvious effort Klutz partly recovered his composure. 'I get these little turns sometimes,' he explained. 'Heart trouble, you know. Just leave me alone. I shall be all right.' He said this in a way clearly intended to discourage further overtures.

Biggles, who had of course seen all this, strolled over to the kiosk and bought a copy of the same paper. He looked at the front page, and without speaking or changing countenance, handed it to Ginger, whose eyes, scanning the page, stopped at the only news item that could have affected Klutz to an extent to cause shock. 'Financier murdered,' was the bold head-line. 'Death on luxury yacht. Last night, Mr. Nestor Janescu, who arrived at Alexandria recently in his famous yacht *Silvanus*, was shot dead by an unknown assailant who appears to have swum out to the vessel. The reason for the murder remains a mystery. Investigations are proceeding. Meanwhile the death of a man so well known in big financial circles is likely to have a sharp effect on world stock markets.'

Ginger handed the paper back to Biggles without a word, but with his eyes conveyed that he understood.

Klutz sat still in his seat, staring at the ground in front of him.

Up to the time the departure of the east-bound plane was announced over the loud-speakers it seemed that they were to be the only passengers. They assumed that Klutz was going. But at the last moment, looking a trifle hot and bothered, in walked Algy and Bertie. Ginger smiled lugubriously. He would have said that Bertie needed no make-up to make him look like an English tourist, but with monocle in eye, camera over shoulder and a well-labelled valise in his hand, he was the continental caricature of one.

102

'By Jove, old boy, we jolly nearly missed the old bus that time,' he told Algy loudly as they hurried to the booking office. Looking over his shoulder at Biggles and Ginger he went on: 'I say, you fellers, just see that beastly plane doesn't go without us.'

Even Klutz half-smiled at this exhibition of British tourism as he got up and went out to where the machine was waiting, engines idling. Biggles and Ginger followed. As they took their seats Algy and Bertie were shown to theirs by the stewardess. There were no other passengers. The door was closed. The engines bellowed, and leaving a cloud of dust swirling behind it the east-bound plane swept into a sky unbroken by a cloud.

To Ginger there was something unreal about the long flight that followed. For the first time they were all in the same plane without being able to speak to each other; for Biggles had, by a warning frown in the direction of Klutz, indicated the position, although, as they too had seen the Air-Commodore's photographs, there was reason to hope that they also had recognized him. Bertie did a lot of talking to Algy, all of an inconsequential nature, but the three parties kept to themselves. Klutz had sunk into his seat, busy with thoughts which, judging from his expression, were not of the brightest.

During the halt at Tripoli to refuel, Algy and Bertie got out, as they said, to stretch their legs. This was the chance for which Biggles had waited, and Biggles and Ginger followed hoping to get in a word. But Klutz, too, got out, and was never out of earshot, although this, Biggles was sure, was entirely fortuitous, for he couldn't have suspected anything.

Algy and Bertie must have been as disappointed as Biggles at this frustration. Algy made a business of

103

checking the time and entering it in his notebook as if he were keeping a log of the trip. Biggles, knowing he couldn't be serious about this, guessed the purpose, and took care to follow him up the steps in the machine when the time came for departure. Ginger put himself between Biggles and Klutz, who therefore did not see the slip of paper pass from Algy to Biggles.

Not until they were in the air did Biggles read the message, and then he did so under cover of his newspaper, holding it so that Ginger, in the next seat, could see it too.

All Algy had written was: 'All as planned. Marcel okay.'

Biggles wrote on the margin of his newspaper: 'Aladdin's Lamp. Stretta Albani. Maybe hotel first. Watch. Destroy this.' Some time later he yawned, and made as if to throw the paper aside. Then, changing his mind, looking at Algy he said loudly: 'Want the morning paper?'

'Thanks,' said Algy, and took the paper.

Klutz, still deep in thought, gave no sign that he had heard.

After reading the message, under cover of his seat Algy tore off the margin, rolled it into a pill, put it in his mouth and chewed it to pulp.

The plane droned on through an atmosphere made bumpy by the scorching sun above and rolling sand dunes below.

It was evening when they touched down at Alexandria, and after the customary routine found themselves outside the airport buildings. Biggles and Ginger, who had of course kept together, would have gone off without a word to their fellow-passengers. But Klutz, who by this time had recovered from his 'attack,' had followed them. 'If you gentlemen don't know your way about I can recommend a comfortable hotel,' he said. 'It is the Continentale, in the North Crescent Square. The proprietor will take care of you,' he added meaningly.

'Thank you, sir. We'll take your advice,' answered Biggles. 'Can we give you a lift?' he enquired, as the next taxi on the line drew up to them.

'No thanks. I have some calls to make,' said Klutz, without moving.

Biggles was still hoping for a word with Algy, but as Klutz obviously intended to see them off, and there was no excuse for lingering, he repeated the address to the taxi driver and got into the vehicle.

Ginger drew a deep breath at finding themselves alone at last. 'Thank goodness we can talk now,' he muttered. 'I found that trip an awful strain. You're really going to this hotel Klutz gave us?'

'We should be fools to go anywhere else. Raban said we should be told where to go. No doubt there's a good reason for sending us to the Continentale and we can guess what it is. I'll bet the boss is on the pay-roll. We'll park our kit, have a wash and a meal, and go on to the club.'

'What about Algy and Bertie?'

'Not so loud. Our driver may be on the pay-roll, too. I'm hoping Algy will watch where we go. This seems to be it.'

The hotel turned out to be a small but much more pretentious establishment than Ginger had imagined. He had expected a cheap place in a back street, but this was something very different. The Square itself was spacious, the centre being occupied by several rows of tall, stately palms, under which, at intervals, wooden seats of the 'park' type had been placed, presumably for the convenience of residents, or visitors staying at one of the several hotels that over-looked the square.

There was nothing particularly imposing about the outside of the Continentale, although it was obviously well kept; but as soon as they were through the swing doors, it was apparent that they were in, if not the luxury class, something near it. The place was strangely quiet. There was nobody in the well-carpeted, tastefully-furnished lounge. However, as soon as Biggles touched the reception bell, an immaculately-dressed man, presumably the proprietor, appeared. He was smooth-skinned and swarthy. Ginger judged him to be either an Egyptian or a Turk. His manner was courteous—rather too courteous, thought Ginger—as with an ingratiating smile he informed them, in answer to Biggles's question, that he could provide them with accommodation. He had two excellent rooms, adjacent, on the first floor, over-looking the square. And in this, Ginger had presently to admit, he had not lied.

No sooner had the man gone back down the stairs than Biggles was in Ginger's room, a finger on his lips. 'Careful what you say,' he breathed. 'There may be dictaphones. If ever a place had a phony atmosphere, this has. No register to sign; no visitors' book. Did you notice the way that fellow stared at our badges? He was taking our numbers. This is all part of the outfit, run for members, so watch your step. Apart from ourselves I believe there's no one else in the place. Listen!' Biggles opened the door wide. There wasn't a sound. The place was as silent as a tomb. 'All right,' he went on in a normal voice. 'We'll have a bath and then go out to have something to eat. Afterwards we'll go on to the club.'

Ginger, who was looking through the window,

touched him on the arm and pointed. Bertie was sauntering through the palms. Reaching a seat nearly opposite he sat down and opened a newspaper.

'Good,' whispered Biggles.

'Are you going to speak to him?'

'Not now. It's too dangerous. After dark, perhaps.'

An hour later, when they went out, the seat was vacant.

'He was letting us know he was about,' said Biggles. 'He knew it wouldn't do to stay there too long. But he may still be watching.'

They soon found a restaurant, where they had a welcome meal, watching the door, thinking Algy or Bertie might follow them in. But they did not appear, which suggested that they, too, were not taking any chances.

'There's one thing that puzzles me about this,' remarked Ginger. 'Why, if the gang runs the hotel, do they use the club. Why have two places?'

'I've been thinking about that myself,' answered Biggles. 'I can see two or three reasons—aside from the obvious possibility that the club may not have sleeping accommodation. Alexandria is a sort of general headquarters. The hotel is maintained as a respectable establishment. But the gang probably employs all sorts of people, including some real toughs. They would need a rendezvous, but it wouldn't do for them to use the hotel. They meet at the club. I'd say most of the people who use the club don't even know of the hotel. So if anything went wrong, or someone squealed and the club was raided, the hotel wouldn't be affected.'

'I see,' murmured Ginger. 'The hotel for the upper crust and the club for the riff-raff.'

'That's about it,' agreed Biggles. 'Let's go and have a look.'

They found the club by the simple expedient of calling a taxi and telling the driver to take them there. The driver said he knew the place—well. From the leer he gave them Ginger suspected that what he knew of it was not to its credit. Biggles paid him off under a hanging oriental lamp outlined in neon tubes.

Entering, they were met by a wave of hot air, a haze of Turkish tobacco smoke, and an enormous black man dressed in a barbarous costume. A tall turban on his head served to increase his height. He looked at their badges, grinned, and motioned them on.

The room in which they now found themselves was a fairly large one, with small tables near the walls to leave an open space in the middle for entertainers— or so it appeared, for they were just in time to see the end of a snake-charming act. Most of the tables were occupied, chiefly by men wearing the now-familiar club badge which, Ginger now realized, was a small replica of the one that hung outside the establishment. However, they found a vacant place. No sooner were they seated than a sleek, dark-skinned waiter, with a fez on his head, appeared, and put a bottle of champagne on the table.

'I didn't order that,' said Biggles.

The waiter looked surprised.

'Take it away.'

The waiter looked hard at their badges and obeyed with alacrity. They watched him go through a door marked 'Staff Only'.

From this there presently emerged a short, stout, unhealthy-looking white man of about fifty, whose skin looked as if it hadn't seen daylight for a long time. What his nationality was Ginger didn't attempt to guess, either then or when, with a great show of affability, he came over and spoke to them. Ginger knew the type: overfed, over-indulgent in every form of vice, over everything except clean living. A man can be fat and still be a jolly good fellow; but this sort, spending his life in vitiated air and electric light, common in every Mediterranean port of any size, reminded him of one of those maggots that thrive on corruption. What astonished him was that the war-mongering syndicate could put the slightest trust in him; for that the man was one of the organization was made apparent by the badge he wore. But perhaps the big men, the brains of the gang, didn't know personally every man they employed, brooded Ginger morosely. That Biggles liked the fellow no more than he did was clear from his expression.

'So you get here, eh,' was the greeting the man gave them. 'My name's Charlie. Everyone calls me Charlie. Dat goes for you. Have a drink.'

'No thanks,' declined Biggles in a flat sort of voice. 'We've just had our dinner.'

'Okay chum. Just order what you like. It's on de house.'

Biggles took a cigarette from his case. 'Listen, Charlie. We're here on business. At least, I thought that was the idea. Can we get on with it? If not, how long do we have to stay?'

Charlie frowned. 'What's de hurry. Summat wrong with de house?'

'For those who like this sort of joint I'd say it's just about perfect,' answered Biggles evenly.

'And what don't *you* like about it?'

'I don't like the noise, I don't like the smell, and I don't like the look of some of your customers,' answered Biggles. 'No offence meant,' he went on quickly. 'I'm just trying to tell you nicely that this sort of entertainment isn't my cup of tea.'

'You like Sunday-school, mebbe,' sneered Charlie.

'The atmosphere of one would be a little less— shall we say, nauseating.'

Charlie glared. 'Den why you come here?'

'Because I was sent here, and I obey orders. You'd better do the same. Now, how about it. I've come a long way and I'm tired.'

Without answering Charlie turned away to where, alone, a young man sat regarding them with an expressionless face. A brief conversation ensued, at the end of which Charlie went out through the staff door and the young man came over to them. He wore the usual badge. His number was twenty-nine, from which Ginger judged, compared with their own numbers, he had been in the organization for some time. Speaking with a queer foreign accent which Ginger could not place he enquired coldly: 'What's the idea upsetting Charlie?'

'If he's upset that's his affair,' replied Biggles. 'I told him if he had anything to say to get on with it. My idea of fun isn't to sit here all night swilling cheap champagne. I'm tired, anyway.'

Number twenty-nine relaxed a little. 'You come long way?'

'Yes.'

'You see my friend Voss I think. Why not he come. He's late.'

'Voss won't be coming,' said Biggles.

'Not come? Why?'

'He's dead.'

Number twenty-nine stared.

110

'The French shot us down as we were taking off,' went on Biggles. 'We came on by the regular service.'

'So. You stay at Continentale?'

'Yes.'

Twenty-nine nodded. 'I come here to fetch you. We go in the morning early.'

'How?'

'Fly. Be at airport tomorrow morning at six and not be late. You see me standing by a Beechcraft Bonanza* outside hangar number three. Just walk over and get in.'

'Suppose somebody stops us?'

Twenty-nine looked at them through half-closed eyes. 'With those badges! No. No one stop you.'

'Anything else?'

'No.'

'Any reasons why we shouldn't know where we're going.'

'Plenty. Maybe you see when you get there—maybe not. Have a drink?'

'No thanks.'

'Please yourself.' Twenty-nine got up and returned to his table.

Biggles and Ginger got up and went out.

---

* A single-engined monoplane, seating 4–6 passengers in an enclosed cabin. Built in the USA.

Chapter 10
One Man's War

'Phew!' breathed Ginger, when they were outside. 'I'm not sorry to be out of that dive.'

'It was a bit of a stinker,' agreed Biggles. 'We'll walk back to the hotel to get some clean air into our lungs. There's a chance we may find Algy or Bertie under the palms. We shall have to check that we're not being shadowed.'

They had not gone far when Ginger, after making a pretence of tying his shoe-lace, announced that they were in fact being followed.

'We'll see who it is,' said Biggles, taking the next side turning and then standing still.

A minute later the follower appeared. It was Algy.

'Keep going,' Biggles told him. 'We'll check there's nobody behind you. See you in the Square under the palms.'

Algy went on.

Biggles waited for five minutes, when, satisfied that all was well, they went on and did not stop again until they were standing in the black shadows of the palms not quite opposite the hotel. Algy appeared with Bertie.

'I left Bertie keeping an eye on the hotel while I watched you to the club,' explained Algy. 'How are things going?'

'Pretty well. We move off in the morning, by air, for an unknown destination. All I can tell you is, the machine is a Beechcraft Bonanza. We join our pilot at six in the morning outside number three hangar. I'm afraid it's no use you trying to follow us even if you could get hold of an aircraft. Where are you staying?'

'At the Napoli. It's next door but one to the Continentale. Run by an Italian. Quite comfortable. As a matter of fact we tried to get into the Continentale, taking it to be a genuine hotel, but were told by that suave piece of work in the reception hall that they were full up.'

'He didn't want you there. I don't think there's a soul in the place except ourselves. It's part of the set-up.'

'I saw a Rolls drop somebody there about an hour ago,' put in Bertie. 'Couldn't see who it was. I don't think he came out. The car didn't wait.'

'I'll remember it,' acknowledged Biggles. 'What happened at the Villa Mimosa?'

'Nothing very exciting, except that we found Marcel locked in a top room,' answered Algy. 'They'd threatened him with all sorts of things to try to make him talk; but he kept his mouth shut knowing that they'd do him in as soon as they'd got the information they wanted. The raid was a complete surprise. Joudrier grabbed everybody, but apart from Raban there were only servants there. Klutz must have left earlier. The job was done nice and quietly. We left Joudrier still searching the house. He told us he'd leave men there to pick up any callers. That includes Voudron next time he goes there. He's keeping the whole thing dark until he hears from you.'

'Good work,' said Biggles. 'That closes one rat hole.'

'The gang will soon know what's happened, of course. That should send the balloon up.'

'By that time we should be ready to throw the net over some bigger fish. What about Marcel?'

'We left him with Joudrier when we made a dash to catch your plane at Algiers. He knows your next stop was to be Alex., so he may follow on. He's satisfied that for the time being there'll be no more deserters from the Legion. That's all buttoned up. What about you. Are you going with this bloke in the morning?'

'Of course. I presume we shall be joining the secret squadron.'

'Sounds grim to me. Must you go?'

'We may never find their hide-out if we don't. This is our chance, and we may never get another. When Klutz hears what's happened at Raban's place he'll tighten up on security. All we can do is to follow the trail fast, as far as it goes, hoping that sooner or later we shall get the complete gen. The lines of communication must eventually end at the top men of the syndicate. But it may not be enough simply to know them by name. We've got to get evidence to show what they've been doing. If they've got military aircraft, stolen or otherwise, at their secret establishment, they'll find it hard to explain what they're doing with them. That's why I'm anxious to see their dump. Klutz must be in touch with the big men. By following him you may learn something.'

'Is that what you want us to do.'

'I don't think you could do better. Stay where you are. Try to locate Klutz. If he was tied up with Janescu, the man who was murdered here the other day, he might go to his yacht, *Silvanus*, in the harbour. You noticed the paragraph I marked in the paper I gave you in the plane?'

'Yes.'

114

'Klutz was shaken to the core when he read it. That's why I feel sure Janescu was in this business. If so he'll be one of the top men, which means that the whole thing must have had a severe shake-up. Who killed Janescu, and why, we needn't try to guess. You'd better keep an eye on the airport. Klutz may fly out. Marcel, since he knows we're here, might drift in. That's all I can say now. Stay on at your hotel so that I shall know where to find you, or send a message if that's possible. There's nothing more we can do tonight. We'll go in. Give us a little while before you show yourselves so that should anybody be watching from the windows of the Continentale they won't know we've been talking.'

'Okay. Hope your landings won't be too bumpy.'

With that they parted, Biggles and Ginger going to their hotel, leaving the others still in the shadows.

The outer doors of the Hotel Continentale were closed, which struck Ginger as odd, for it was not particularly late. In any case it might have been supposed that the hotel would keep open all night, with a night porter on duty. However, the door opened at the turn of the handle, revealing that the vestibule behind the glass-panelled swing-doors was in darkness. This struck Ginger as even more queer, for the proprietor, who would know they were out, would hardly expect his guests to grope about for the light switches. They went on through the swing-doors and then stood still. The silence was profound. Too profound, thought Ginger, whose pulses were beginning to tingle. Such silence in any building was unnatural, but in a hotel of some size—in darkness, too—it was uncanny.

Said Biggles, in a low voice: 'Did you happen to notice where the light switches were?'

Ginger answered no, but assuming they would be on the far wall, took a pace forward. His foot came into contact with something soft and yielding. At the same instant Biggles's lighter flicked on. The light it gave was dim, but it was enough to explain the mystery. At Ginger's feet, lying on his back with arms outflung, lay the proprietor.

'Don't move.' Biggles's voice was a whisper.

'Switch the lights on,' pleaded Ginger.

'No.' Biggles walked softly to where the man lay, knelt beside him for a moment, then got up. 'He's had it,' he announced. 'It wasn't long ago, either.'

'I didn't see anyone go in while we were talking to Algy.'

'Nor I.'

'You think . . .'

'Whoever did it may still be in the building.'

'What are you going to do about it?'

'We'll get out. We must. We daren't stay here. If we do we shall be in a spot.'

Ginger could see that. Whether they themselves called the police, or were found in the hotel when someone else did so, they would be questioned, perhaps arrested. They would be back-tracked to Algiers, after which the police would soon discover that they were deserters from the Foreign Legion. What could they say, faced with such an accusation? To tell the truth would expose them to the conspirators for what they were. Clearly, their only hope was to get out while they could.

'Let's get our kit,' said Biggles softly, and started off up the stairs, lighted faintly by moonlight coming through a landing window.

From the top of the staircase a corridor ran the length of the building, with bedrooms on both sides.

116

Their own rooms were nearly at the far end, which, they had learned, was a private suite, although at the time of their arrival it was not occupied.

Before proceeding Biggles paused to listen. Silence, utter and complete, still persisted. Knowing what was in the vestibule made it all the more disturbing, and Ginger found his lips going dry.

He was about to move forward when a door about halfway along the corridor was opened from the inside and a shadowy figure, moving with furtive stealth, emerged, and, without a sound, went on towards the far end.

Ginger froze. It did not occur to him that the intruder was anything but a common thief, who, having killed the proprieter, was going through the rooms looking for valuables. Apparently Biggles thought the same, and decided that it was no affair of theirs. At all events, he stood still while the man went on to the private suite. The intruder opened the door an inch. No light came from inside. He then went in, closing the door behind him.

By this time Ginger was feeling he couldn't get out fast enough. Creeping about any house after dark is somewhat trying to the nerves; but in this sinister atmosphere, with a dead man behind them and his presumed murderer just in front, he found it most unpleasant.

Biggles touched him on the arm and together they tiptoed to their rooms.

It took Ginger only a minute to fling his few toilet things into his bag; and he was on his way out to see if Biggles was ready when his nerves were jolted severely by a gunshot, close but muffled.

Biggles must have heard it, for he came out. Simultaneously the end door was flung open and a man

117

dashed out in such a hurry that they came into collision with sufficient violence to send them both reeling. The man, recovering with a gasp, raised his arm. The hand held a gun. Ducking, Biggles dived for his legs, and they both went down with a crash.

This sudden frenzied action after the previous silence was shattering, and Ginger's movements were inspired more by instinct than reasoned deliberation. Biggles and the man were on the floor. Whether the man was holding Biggles, or Biggles holding the man, in the dim light it was impossible to tell. But Ginger knew the man had a gun, so it was obvious that Biggles was in imminent danger of being shot.

Going to the rescue he found that Biggles was holding down the arm that held the gun, so that the muzzle was turned away from him. Ginger knelt on the arm and with some difficulty twisted the gun from a vice-like grip; but not before it had gone off, deafening him, half-blinding him with its flash, and bringing down plaster from the ceiling.

'Quit fighting or I'll knock your block off,' he said fiercely, seeing now that they were dealing with a white man, and not, as he thought it might be, an Arab.

The man's reply was a violent wrench that tore him free from Biggles, so that he reeled backwards through the door of the suite, which was wide open. Biggles snatched the gun from Ginger and covered him. 'Pack up,' he rasped. 'And don't make any more noise. I'm as anxious to get out of this place as you are.'

The man, panting, torn and dishevelled, backed farther into the room. Biggles followed him, and finding the light switch flicked it on. 'Stand still,' he ordered. 'We don't belong here. We're on our way out.'

'With those badges? Pah! You can't kid me, you rats,' grated the man, who seemed to be beside himself with fury. He glanced at the window as if contemplating a flying leap through it.

But it was not this that made Ginger start. Sprawled across the floor, in pyjamas, was a man. It was Klutz. As a result of the scuffle Ginger had forgotten the first shot. Now he understood.

Biggles's face set in hard lines as he looked down. 'Did you do this?' he asked sternly.

'Sure I did it,' boasted the man viciously. 'And that oily Armenian crook downstairs. They had it coming to 'em.'

'Did you by any chance kill Janescu?' asked Biggles.

'Yeah. And I'll get the rest of the whole dirty bunch if I live long enough. You too. You wear their flaming badge.'

Ginger began to wonder if the man was sane. With his face flushed and his eyes glinting, he was obviously in a state of high excitement, if nothing worse. He didn't appear to have been drinking.

'Now just a minute,' said Biggles quietly. 'Take it easy, and don't jump to conclusions.'

'Bah! You've got your badges. Go on. Why don't you plug me, you murdering swine.'

'If you'd pull yourself together instead of blathering you'd realize that if we were in the racket we'd have shot you by now.'

The man stared. This, apparently, had not occurred to him. But he must have seen that the argument made sense.

'I don't know who you are or why you're doing this;

119

but since I'm trying to do the same thing, in a legal way, I'm more than interested,' said Biggles.

'Who are you, anyway?'

'Suppose I told you we were detectives from London?'

The man looked incredulous. 'Then why are you wearing those badges?'

'It shouldn't be hard to guess that.'

'Where did you get 'em?'

'We were given them. Without them we couldn't have got where we hope to get. That's why we wear them. They got us in here. Now we're on our way out before someone discovers that you've turned the place into a shambles.'

'You're not arresting me?'

'I've more important things to do than fiddle with a man who's bent on suicide, anyway. You can go when you like and where you like as far as I'm concerned. Of course, if you're prepared to talk I'm ready to listen. Can you tell us anything?'

'Plenty,' answered the man grimly. 'You see, before I got wise to the racket I used to wear one of those badges.'

'I see,' returned Biggles slowly. 'Now you're trying to mop up the gang single-handed.'

'You've got it, brother. And I'm not doing so badly.'

'From the way you talk you're an American.'

'Sure I am. The name's Lindsay—Cy Lindsay—if that means anything to you.'

'It doesn't, admitted Biggles. 'But never mind. Go on. How did you come to get mixed up with this lot?'

'I used to be a top grade chauffeur-mechanic in New York. That's where I was taken on by Pantenelli.'

'Do you mean Fabiano Pantenelli?'

'That's right. The rubber market boss.'

'So he's in it?'

'Up to the eyebrows. I'll come clean. I got into a spot of trouble and lost my job. Along comes a feller with a wad of dollars and offers me a better one. It was to drive Pantenelli and keep my mouth shut about anything I saw. I was his driver for close on two years—not always in the States. That's how I got to know Janescu and Festwolder. Festwolder sells guns to mugs to shoot each other. Hugo Festwolder! He was one of the skunks who backed Hitler but was wise enough not to be seen in the game—oh, he was wise, that one. But I'll get him.'

'What about Klutz?'

'He organized the dirty work. Well, he's finished organizing. The Committee of Three. That's what he called his bosses, Janescu, Festwolder and Pantenelli. Now it's a Committee of Two, and they'll need a new general manager to fix the next war. I must have been dumb not to tumble to their game before I did. War! I called it a game, but it's big business. By that time I was deep in, and was thinking of a way out when I heard my kid brother had been killed in Korea*. That finished me. I saw red. Yeah! That's what I saw. Red. I'd been working for the smart guys who were piling up dollars by sending kids to their deaths. I swore I'd get even with 'em.'

'Why didn't you go to the police?'

'What police? Do you think I wanted to be bumped off? Listen brother. This racket covers half the world. If I'd squealed Klutz would have known about it inside five minutes. No. I decided I'd play their own game. War. And I'd fight it single-handed. I'm not doing so bad.'

* The Korean War.

121

Biggles shook his head. 'You can't go on doing this.'

'I'll go on till they stop me.'

'What brought you to Alexandria?'

'Janescu's yacht. You can't move a yacht without it being known. A ship like the *Silvanus* is news. I've been aboard her often. That was their weakness. They daren't meet anywhere ashore for fear of people wondering what was going on. The stock markets have their spies, you know. So they used to meet on the yacht, where everyone was on their pay-roll, of course, and no risk of eavesdroppers. When the *Silvanus* came here I guessed what was cooking and came along hoping to catch 'em all on board. But I was too early. Only Janescu was there. I guessed Klutz would be here. This is his usual hang-out in this part of the world. I'm glad I got him, anyway. Maybe it's better that way.'

'Why?'

'It'll make it easier to get the others.'

'How do you work that out?'

'Because now Pantenelli and Festwolder will have to come into the open themselves instead of skulking out of sight like a couple o' coyotes. They hatched the plots. All they had to do then was pass the word to Klutz. He did the actual work, the organizing; and I must say he did it well. He'd been at it a long time. The gang was his, really. The Committee paid the bills. Now Klutz has gone, what are they going to do?'

'Need they do anything?'

'Betcha life they need. They daren't just slide out. What do you think would happen if the gang didn't get paid? They'd squeal. Or some of 'em would. It only needs one of 'em to open his mouth and the game would be up. Pantenelli and Festwolder know that. They know they've got a tough crowd to handle.

122

Klutz could handle them. But he's finished. So what? Pantenelli and Festwolder will have to do his work, and they'll have to move fast, because some of the boys at the Valley are getting sore anyhow.'

'You think Pantenelli and Festwolder are in Alex. now?'

'Sure to be.'

'What do they look like?'

'Festwolder's a big feller with red hair and big red whiskers. Pantenelli is a little slick type. Looks like he might be a Mexican dance band conductor.'

'Have you been here before?'

'Of course I have. Didn't I say I'd been everywhere with 'em? You see, I've still got my badge. I keep changing the number. It still gets me places. They can't stop it unless they change all the badges and that would be a big job. There are hundreds of 'em. I don't go to the club any more. Charlie knows me by sight. I suppose you've been there? Everyone goes through it.'

'We were there tonight.'

'One day I'm going to clean that place up with a stick or two of dynamite,' swore Lindsay.

'Now you listen to me,' said Biggles severely. 'I've told you to pack up. You'll do more good, for us as well as yourself, by staying alive.'

'How?'

'By coming forward and giving evidence when this bunch is rounded up.'

'What are you aiming to do next? I mean, where do you go from here?'

'I wish I knew. We're air pilots. We're booked for the gang's secret squadron. We still don't know where it is, but we're being taken there tomorrow morning by a fellow whose number is twenty-nine.'

'Dark chap with a hard face? Little scar on his cheekbone?'

'That's the man.'

'His name's Leffers. Used to be in the Luftwaffe. Went to the States after the war, killed a guy and bolted into the Foreign Legion. That's how they got him into the racket. Deserter. Be careful. He's bad— and tough.'

'Have you been to this secret squadron?'

'No, but I know where-abouts it is because I've met most of the fellers who have.'

'Where is it?'

'Don't ask me what country it's in because I don't know. I shouldn't think anyone knows. I once heard Janescu say he didn't know, and he's got an outfit supposed to be drilling for oil not far away. A chauffeur hears a lot of things, even when it doesn't look as though he's listening.'

'Come to the point. Where is this place?'

'The actual spot is known as the Valley of the Tartars. It's near the beginning of the Bashan Pass, where the borders of Iraq, Persia and Turkey meet—not far from the U.S.S.R. Leffers called it Kurdistan. Awful country, no use to anybody. That's why nobody has ever tried to push out the sheikh, or whatever he is, who claims the district. He's on the committee's payroll. I know that because I heard Pantenelli tell Janescu he was asking for more money. The landmark is an old castle. Amazing place, I believe, as old as the hills. You can't see the machines because they're camouflaged under dust-sheets. Yet according to some fellers the place isn't hard to find. You simply cross Syria and Iraq by following the oil pipe-line to Kirkuk. Then you turn north on a course for a place called

Gelia Dagh. That takes you over it. Are you thinking of going there?'

'I am.'

'Then watch yourselves. If that bunch—and they're mostly deserters from one army or another—get one sniff of what you're doing you'd be out—just like that. They don't argue. They shoot. You get like that when you know you're on the wrong side of the fence. Always on the jump. That gives you an itchy finger. Maybe that's what's wrong with me. What do you reckon I ought to do?'

'That's better,' said Biggles approvingly. 'Have you any money?'

'A little.'

Biggles pulled out his wad and stripped off most of it. 'I'll tell you exactly what I want you to do, and if you're wise you'll do it. Alex. is no place for you. Go straight to the airport. You should just be in time to catch the night airmail to London. Go straight to Scotland Yard and ask for Air-Commodore Raymond. Tell him you've seen me—the name's Bigglesworth. Tell him what you've told me and say we've gone on to the Valley of Tartars. You can also say that Lacey is staying at the Hotel Napoli, next door but one to here. He'll tell you what to do after that. Is that clear?'

'Sure.'

Biggles handed Lindsay his gun. 'I'll let you have this, but don't use it again unless you have to, in self-defence.'

'As you say. But if you go to the Valley of Tartars I shan't reckon on seeing you again. Once you've seen their dump you'll never get out.'

'But what about the flying? What's to stop a man taking off and not going back?'

'To start with they don't let you fly alone. You always

have at least one of the old hands with you until they can trust you—which means until you've done some bombing or shooting. They have guns. You don't. They've other ways of keeping tab on you, too.'

'Well, we've managed so far,' said Biggles. 'Now you'd better get out of here. We'll follow later. I want to see if Klutz has anything interesting in his pockets. If . . .' His voice trailed away at the expression that appeared suddenly on Lindsay's face. His eyes were on the door.

Biggles turned, as did Ginger.

Standing in the doorway, his face pale, his eyes venomous, and his lips compressed to a thin line, was number twenty-nine, Leffers.

Chapter 11
Still Farther East

Leffers's eyes went to Klutz, lying horribly still on the floor. Then with a sort of slow deliberation, they examined the faces of the others in turn. They came to rest on Lindsay. 'So you've been talking,' he said, in a dry, brittle voice.

Lindsay was not intimidated. Indeed the words seemed to make his passion flare up again. 'So what?' he spat.

Ginger was inclined to think that Leffers didn't notice that Lindsay had a gun in his hand or he wouldn't have been so foolish as to try to pull his own. Be that as it may, Leffers's gun was only half out of his pocket when Lindsay's crashed.

Only by a slight twitch did Leffers show that he had been hit. His right hand, holding his automatic, dropped an inch at a time. The gun fell with a thud. Then, in a silence that was almost tangible, he sank slowly to the floor, at the finish sliding forward like a swimmer in deep water. With an expression of pained surprise on his face he lay still under a faint reek of blue cordite smoke.

The silence was broken by Lindsay. There was something unreal, artificial, about his tone of voice. 'That's another,' he said.

Biggles was angry. 'I've no time for Leffers but you shouldn't have done that,' he snapped.

Lindsay made a gesture of helplessness. 'What else

was there to do?' he asked, almost plaintively. 'Stand still and let him knock us off one at a time?'

Biggles shrugged. 'I suppose you're right,' he admitted with reluctance. 'But don't stand there,' he went on. 'Get out.'

'What about you? I'm willing to take the rap . . .'

'Rap nothing. Get going. I've told you what to do. I've something to do here before I leave.'

Lindsay nodded. He thrust the gun in his pocket and walked away down the corridor without a backward glance.

Ginger looked at Biggles questioningly.

'I'm going to see what these two have in their pockets,' Biggles told him. 'We may never get such another chance. Keep *cave.*'

Ginger turned to watch the corridor.

Biggles was busy behind him for about five minutes. Then he said: 'That's all. Come on.'

In a silence as profound as when they had entered the building, but now even more menacing, they went down the stairs, out of the door, and crossed the road swiftly.

'I expect they'll have gone,' said Biggles as they reached the palms, referring of course to Algy and Bertie.

They were still there, however, much to Biggles's satisfaction.

'We heard shooting and thought we'd better hang on for a bit,' explained Algy. 'What was it all about?'

In as few words as possible Biggles told him what had happened in the hotel, passing on the information Lindsay had given him, including particulars of the location of the secret squadron.

'Look here, I say old boy,' protested Bertie in a

shocked voice. 'If you're going to tootle around leaving a trail of corpses kicking about—'

'I didn't make the corpses,' Biggles pointed out with asperity. 'That American is fighting mad. I wished him further, I can tell you.'

'Where's he gone?'

'London, I hope. I told him to report to Raymond.'

'I'd have given him a second gun and told him to carry on,' asserted Algy. 'He was doing our job for us. In bumping off two of the leading war-makers he's thinned the opposition by fifty per cent. I call that pretty good going.'

'By Jove! And how right you are,' put in Bertie. 'Absolutely. I'm with you every time. After all, I mean to say, blokes who make war haven't a grouse if somebody makes war on them. I'm all for those who live by the sword dying by the jolly old sword, and all that sort of thing. Usually it's the other bloke who gets—'

'Pipe down,' pleaded Biggles. 'This is no time for fatuous arguments. What this fellow Lindsay has done is push us out of our billets. He's worked for the Syndicate so he has only himself to blame for what's happened. Of course, he doesn't see it like that. What's really biting him is remorse, because his brother was killed. So have a lot of other people's brothers been killed, but they don't rush about with a gun in each hand. Still, Lindsay has given us a lot of useful information so we shouldn't complain. I thought this show might finish with some fireworks but I wasn't prepared for anything like this.'

'It must have been Lindsay we saw come out just now.'

'I told him to push off while I had a look to see what Klutz and Leffers had in their pockets.'

'Find anything?'

'I don't really know yet. I'm anxious to have a look at one or two things I brought away. Which brings me to the question, where are we going for the night? I'm not going to walk the streets.'

'Why not come to our hotel? I'm sure there's plenty of room.'

'We'll try it. There's going to be a nice how-do-you-do at the Continentale in the morning, when the police hear about what's inside. But by that time I hope to be away.'

'You're really going to this Valley of Tartars place?'

'Of course.'

'Can you find it.'

'I'm going to try. From Lindsay's description it shouldn't be too difficult. It's a fair run from here. Speaking from memory it must be between eight hundred and a thousand miles.'

'What'll they say when you roll up without Leffers?'

'I shall tell them the truth—that he was shot in the hotel by a man named Lindsay. They must know all about Lindsay so the story should prove our sincerity.'

'They'll ask how you found the place.'

Biggles smiled faintly. 'Obviously, Leffers told me before he died. Incidentally, I could kick myself for not guessing that Leffers was staying at the hotel. He as good as told me so.'

'I can only hope you get away with it,' returned Algy dubiously.

'Let's go over to your place and see if they can fix us up,' said Biggles.

As Algy had anticipated, there was no difficulty about getting into the Napoli. They did not go to bed, but all forgathering in Algy's room they spent the rest of the night—or rather, the early hours of the morning—discussing the situation and going through the things Biggles had taken from the pockets of Klutz and Leffers. Both had been careful about what they carried, and the only item of practical use was a flimsy tracing of the route from Egypt to the Valley of Tartars, which presumably Leffers had prepared for his own guidance. A compass course had been jotted on one corner, but the objective had not been named, so the map would have meant nothing to anyone who did not know the facts of the case. Among the things Biggles had brought was Leffers badge, in order, as he said, to prevent the police from attaching any significance to it, as they might if other badges were found in the hotel, which was well within the bounds of possibility. They didn't want the police, who were likely to do more harm than good, barging in at the present stage of things. Still less did he want to be picked up by them if, assuming that the murders were the fruits of gang warfare, they started to round up for questioning everyone wearing an Aladdin Lamp badge.

At five o'clock, Biggles, who had decided to adhere to Leffers's time-table, said they had better see about moving off, as at such an early hour it might take them some time to find transport to the airport. The false dawn was just touching the eastern sky with a grey finger.

There had been no sounds of activity from the direction of the nearby Continentale, and Ginger, taking a cautious peep out of the window, made the surprising discovery that there was neither a policeman nor a police car in sight. This, they all agreed, was curious, the first impression being that the murders had not yet been discovered. But Biggles soon took a different view. He pointed out that there must have been servants in the house, for a man like Klutz was

131

hardly likely to make his own bed and get his own morning coffee. Even if he had arrived late arrangements for this would have been made. It seemed likely, he averred, that the staff, who would be on the top floor, and for that reason had not been awakened by the shooting, were still in bed. Another possibility was, on finding the bodies they had panicked and fled, knowing that police enquiries, which they would find embarrassing, would follow. Not that it mattered, said Biggles, for they themselves had finished with the hotel.

Soon afterwards, with Ginger, leaving the others to follow—one to the docks and the other to the airport—he set off for the business quarter of the city where he hoped to find a cab. In this he was successful, with the result that they arrived a little before time.

The Beechcraft Bonanza, wearing civil American registration marks, was standing just outside Number Three hangar just as Leffers had said it would be. Only one official intercepted them, and he, after one glance at their badges, didn't even speak, but with an almost imperceptible nod continued walking.

'He's another one,' muttered Ginger. 'This thing begins to look like one of those master-mind organizations that Edgar Wallace used to write about.'

'That's exactly what it is,' answered Biggles. 'In this case, though, we're dealing with a racket that thinks in millions, not the comparative chicken-feed to be made out of bank-busting, blackmail, and so on.'

They found a mechanic leaning against the far side of the aircraft. He looked at them, then beyond them. 'Where's twenty-nine?' he asked.

'He's not coming,' replied Biggles. 'We're going on alone.'

'Not coming,' echoed the man suspiciously. 'Why not?'

'Because he's dead,' said Biggles shortly.

'I was talking to him last night.'

'So was I, but that doesn't make him alive this morning.'

'What happened?'

'He was shot.'

'That Lindsay again?'

'Why think that?'

'I'm told to watch for him. He must have gone nuts. They say it was him who killed Janescu.'

'You know Lindsay?'

'Course I know him. He's been here scores of times.'

'What matters more, is this machine fuelled up?'

'You're all right for everything. I saw to it myself.'

'In that case we may as well get off,' said Biggles casually.

'What about the other man?'

'What other man?'

'There's another passenger. She carries four.'

For a second Biggles was taken aback. 'Leffers didn't say anything to me about another man.'

'He told me he was taking three new men. Two Englishmen and a German—a man he knew back home. Served under him in the war. He's going out to take charge.'

'I thought Klein was in charge.'

'He was. He isn't now. They say he got caught in a dust storm and flew into the ground coming in.'

'So this new man is going to take Klein's place.'

'That's what Leffers said.'

'What's his number?'

'I dunno. Leffers didn't say. He told me his name. It was von Stalhein—or something like that.'

Not a muscle of Biggle's face moved. 'Well, he isn't here so we'll get off.'

'Six was the time.' The man looked at the control tower clock. 'It ain't quite six yet.'

'It's near enough. He isn't coming or he'd be here by now.'

'What's the hurry?'

'I'll tell you, but keep it to yourself. The police are likely to be here any minute to check on passengers leaving.'

'Why?'

'Klutz was shot last night—same time as Leffers.'

The man looked shocked. 'Where was this?'

'At the Continentale. The police are bound to watch every exit from the city and I'd rather not answer questions. You'd better get out of their way, too.'

'I'd say so. Okay.'

Biggles climbed into the aircraft. Ginger followed, trying to pretend—not very successfully—that there was no hurry. Actually, there was every reason to hurry, and he knew it; for during the last part of Biggles's conversation with the mechanic he had seen a Rolls draw up at the tarmac. Three men got out. Two he did not know, but there was no mistaking the lean military figure of the other, who walked with a slight limp. It was their old arch enemy, Erich von Stalhein, one time of the Wilhelmstrasse* but more recently

---

* Headquarters of the German Secret Service.

employed by operators of the Cold War behind the Iron Curtain*.

'Get cracking,' Ginger told Biggles urgently. 'Look who's here.'

'I saw,' murmured Biggles evenly. 'The pace is getting a bit warm, isn't it.'

'It's getting too hot,' declared Ginger. 'And it'll be hotter still if von Stalhein learns who's in this kite.'

'There's only one thing on my mind,' said Biggles, as, getting the okay from the control tower, he eased the throttle open.

'You mean, when von Stalhein arrives to take over.'

'By then, with any luck, we should be on our way home. No. I'm thinking of radio. If Alexandria is in touch with the Valley of Tartars on a private wavelength we may find things a bit difficult. That's the first thing we must find out when we get there.'

'I should say,' said Ginger, speaking very deliberately, 'if that turns out to be the case we shan't have to trouble to find out. We shall be told—with nice new nickel bullets.'

Biggles grinned. 'Made by the War Syndicate.'

'We should have brought our guns.'

'We couldn't have got into the Legion with guns in our pockets. I told you that at the start.'

Ginger said no more.

The Beechcraft climbed higher into the blue dome overhead as the air, already feeling the heat of the sun, began to rock her.

Presently Biggles said: 'You realized who that was with von Stalhein?'

* Common term used to describe dividing line between capitalist western countries and the Communist Eastern European countries, 1948–1989.

'I was wondering . . . if it was . . .'

'From Lindsay's description it was Pantenelli and Festwolder. It looks as if he was right when he said they'd have to do their own dirty work, and get cracking with it, too.'

'We've got their machine, anyway,' said Ginger comfortingly.

Chapter 12
The Valley of the Tartars

For five hours the aircraft bumped its way through sun-tortured air over the oldest civilized lands on earth; lands where history fades into the dim Past, where civilizations have come and gone leaving only a few carved stones to show they ever existed; lands where every mile had its Biblical associations, where every trail had echoed in turn to the tramp of marching armies, Assyrian, Persian, Egyptian, Greek, Roman, and, in later years, Turkish, British, French, German and Arab; the lands where Moses and his weary followers had sought the Promised Land.

Milk and Honey there may have been then, but today for the most part these are lands of waterless deserts, vast expanses of sterile earth, of sand, volcanic ash and hard-baked pebbly clay, sometimes flat, sometimes rolling in long hideous dunes, where the only thing that can endure the flaying of the merciless sun is the everlasting camelthorn. Sometimes the sand gleams like gold dust. Sometimes even the bed-rock has been torn apart by the convulsions of long-forgotten storms. And there are places where sinister black stains show where the core of the earth has burst through its crust to form the bitumen wells that supplied the mortar for the walls of ancient Babylon thousands of years before the word cement was coined.

The sky is the colour of burnished steel.

Between it and the shimmering wastes below, the

aircraft fought its way, sometimes rising and falling on invisible hundred-foot waves of thin, tormented air.

At first, with the blue Mediterranean to the north and Sinai to the south, the flying had not been such hard work, but by the time they had crossed Palestine, with Transjordan and the Great Syrian Desert ahead, the sun had climbed high, and pilotage in a light machine was anything but pleasant. Over Iraq Biggles had no difficulty in picking up the pipe-line which, running as straight as a railway with guard-houses at intervals, took them to the Tigris. Still the pipe-line ran on, but as soon as the oil derricks of Kirkuk came into sight (the Biblical Place of the Burning Fiery Furnace) Biggles turned north towards the final objective.

To the north and east now the horizon was cut into a serrated chaos by the thousand peaks of Kurdistan— still the home of untamed tribes, untouched, unchanged by the advance of Western Civilization. Which of the mountains was Gelia Dagh, wondered Ginger, who was watching the falling petrol gauge with some anxiety. One thing was certain. They couldn't get back without a fresh supply of fuel. Biggles was, he knew, breaking the first rule of desert travel, which is never to go beyond 'the point of no return'. That is to say, beyond the endurance range of the vehicle, whether it be surface craft or aircraft. Apparently he was determined to go on, trusting to finding petrol and oil available at the Valley of the Tartars. It was a reasonable assumption, always supposing that they did not fail to locate the place. In that event they hadn't a hope of getting out alive, for they had none of the emergency facilities which were provided for service machines at the time of R.A.F.

occupation—radio that could pin-point their position to armoured cars stationed at strategic points.

They were, in fact, some time in finding the particular valley they sought, but after losing height and circling for a while it was the old castle, its crumbling battlements silhouetted for a moment against the sky, that gave them its position. An orange-coloured piece of material was presently put out by the people there, but by that time wheel marks in the sandy ground, which could not be obliterated or camouflaged except by natural dust storms, had revealed the actual landing area.

Five minutes later the Beechcraft's wheels were running in the grooves. After the machine had run to a standstill Biggles taxied on to where some men were sitting under and awning near a line of dilapidated-looking tents and a long wooden hutment.

Nothing about the place came up to Ginger's expectations. He had expected something like a proper service station. From what he had seen of the surrounding country he knew that the landscape could be nothing but an arid, dusty, barren scene of hopeless desolation, a waste of rock and sand, fit only to be the abode of snakes and scorpions; and in this he was not mistaken. It could hardly be otherwise, he reflected. Fertile places are occupied, and the secret squadron, by its nature, had to be far from possible observers. The wild hillmen, out of touch with the rest of the world, hardly counted as human beings. How the pilots bore the solitude and lack of amenities he could not imagine. However, he was to learn in due course.

The castle, the only feature in sight, was an imposing building. Standing like a giant defying time on a spur of rock, he quailed at the thought of the plight of the wretched slaves responsible for its construction; for no voluntary labour would have undertaken such a task in such a place. Who had ordered the building of it he did not know, and could not imagine. He had seen similar castles farther south; but those had been built by the Crusaders, near the caravan routes. This was out of the world. Three aircraft, more or less covered by ragged khaki dustsheets, stood in the shade of a nearby escarpment.

There were about a dozen men sitting about waiting for the Beechcraft to switch off. Not one got up to offer a greeting. They were, perhaps, too bored, or too tired, thought Ginger. Their appearance certainly supported that view, for a more scruffy-looking lot of white men he had never seen. Shorts and open-necked shirts, the worse for wear and none too clean, was the common dress. Ginger had half expected to find the garrison in uniforms. Two or three of the men had half-grown beards, and these doubtful adornments, with long hair in need of cutting, did nothing to improve their appearance. None of the men had shaved for days; and if there is one thing more dilatory-looking than long hair it is an unshaven chin. One thing was plain. Something was radically wrong at the air headquarters of the Committee of Three, and discipline, if ever there had been any, had gone by the board.

Said a bearded man, sitting on an oil-drum, as Biggles and Ginger moved into the shade of the awning: 'Where are the cigarettes?'

Biggles, naturally, looked a bit puzzled. 'Cigarettes?'

The man frowned. 'Didn't you bring any?'

'Only what I have in my case.'

'Where's Leffers? He was to bring a stock.'

'If you're waiting for Leffers to bring a supply you'll wait a long time.'

'How so?'

'He's dead.'

This piece of information caused a stir; and consternation, although this obviously was not so much sympathy for the dead man as his failure to produce cigarettes, which were evidently in short supply. There was some swearing.

'He didn't say anything to me about cigarettes,' volunteered Biggles. Which was perfectly true.

'What happened?' he was asked.

'He was shot by someone in the Continentale, in Alex. I saw him at the club.'

'Klein, Voss, now Leffers,' muttered a disreputable-looking youth. 'What's Klutz playing at, leaving us in the cart like this?'

'Klutz isn't playing at anything. He was shot at the same time as Leffers.'

'How come you to know all this?'

'We'd just flown in from Algiers and were in the hotel at the time. We heard the shooting, and seeing what had happened pushed off before the police arrived. We'd met Leffers by appointment at the club. Those were our orders. He told us to meet him at the airport at six. That's all he told us, except about this place. Knowing what had happened we came on alone. What else were we to do? We couldn't go back to Algiers and we daren't stay in Alex.'

'What about the other man—the feller who's to take Klein's place?'

'Leffers didn't say anything to me about that. Would you like me to go back and fetch him?'

There was some sarcastic laughter.

'What's the joke?' asked Biggles.

'We're out of petrol,' was the staggering reply. 'In fact, we're out of everything except bully and biscuits,' added the speaker bitterly.

'Why not do something about it?' suggested Biggles. 'I imagine you've got radio. Why not put an S.O.S. through to Alex.?'

'We had radio but it don't work any more. Klein put it out of action to stop us bleating.'

The story that was now unfolded caused Ginger no great surprise. It was in fact a sequence of natural consequences. In the first place the members of the secret squadron were men of doubtful, it not bad, character. Rebels by nature, it would not take much to upset them. Secondly, there was the soul-destroying location of the airfield with a climate few white men could endure for long without special equipment and amenities.

For a while everything had run on oiled wheels. Klein, with his two trusted lieutenants, Voss and Leffers, had maintained discipline and organized a steady supply of stores—the most important of which, in a nervy, thirsty climate, had been beer and cigarettes. But then Klein's own nerves had broken down and he had taken to drink. In such a situation things had gone quickly from bad to worse. Klein had quarrelled with Voss and Leffers. The men grumbled, saying that Klein was keeping the beer and cigarettes for himself. Morale had crumbled. Klein had taken the output valve from the radio to prevent any of his men from complaining to Alexandria when his back was turned. He carried it in his pocket. He was never sober. He was drunk when he had got into his machine to do a bombing job that had been ordered. That was why he had flown into the hill. The output valve had gone west with him. Voss had flown to Alexandria to report to Klutz, get a new machine and fresh recruits. He hadn't come back. Then Leffers had gone. Now he, too, had been killed. The disgruntled men in the Valley of the Tartars, having faith in Klutz's efficiency, had sat waiting for him to put things right. Now Klutz was dead. Someone suggested that Raban, who was a smart guy, might do something. They knew Raban, from which it appeared that they were deserters from the Foreign Legion.

Ginger could have told them that Raban's activities had also ended. It was clear to him that the squadron was in a bad way. Lindsay, and to some extent themselves, had already struck the Valley a blow that might prove mortal. Its one hope of survival was von Stahlein, who was a disciplinarian, and efficient. The same man might be responsible for their own non-survival should he arrive on the scene while they were there, he reflected ruefully. And without petrol they looked like staying there. The great redeeming factor of the situation was the radio being out of action.

The men were still grumbling about what had happened, most of them blaming Klein. From their conversation Ginger made it out that there were three pilots. The rest were mechanics or camp assistants. They were of mixed nationality, but all spoke either English or French, which they would have learned in the Legion.

'Blaming Klein won't help now,' Biggles pointed out. 'As you've probably realized, we're new. We were promised something a bit different from this.'

'There may be a row about you taking that plane,' said a man. 'It's one of those the Committee keep for their own use.'

'I wasn't to know that. What do you mean by *one* of the Committee's machines? Have they others?'

'How do you suppose they get stores and heavy stuff out to us?'

'I wouldn't know.'

'They keep a Douglas D.C.3* at Alex. for the job,' explained another man. 'Feller named Liebnitz flies it. He's in Alex. now, loading up—that's if *he* ain't been bumped off, too. He was to bring petrol for the next job.'

'What's the idea of keeping you so short of petrol?' asked Biggles.

There was more cynical laughter. Said a man: 'Don't be such a sucker. If there was plenty of petrol left lying loose somebody might go for a ride and not come back. I would, for one. Sitting here day after day, frying like an egg in a pan.'

'We've had a thirsty trip,' remarked Biggles. 'How do we go for water?'

'There's plenty of that—but who wants to drink water in a place like this.'

Biggles shrugged. 'We shall have to drink something or shrivel in this heat.'

'There's a well in the castle.'

'I see,' said Biggles. 'What are you fellows going to do?'

Nobody knew. At all events, nobody answered.

'Sitting here waiting for something that may never come isn't my idea of fun.'

'Okay, wise guy,' growled a big, unshaven fellow. 'You think of something if you're so smart.'

'Somebody will have to go to Alex., and get this mess straightened out.'

'How?'

---

* A twin-engined transport aircraft, carrying 35–40 passengers, or freight. Built in the USA.

144

'I wasn't thinking of walking,' answered Biggles evenly. 'Isn't there an oilfield somewhere near here?'

One of the men laughed harshly. 'You don't dig petrol out of the ground, pal. You get crude oil. They haven't struck it yet, anyhow. They're still drilling. That's what we're supposed to be doing here.'

'I see. Where do you reckon is the nearest place we could get petrol?'

The men looked at each other and agreed it would be Mosul, in Northern Iraq.

'That's about two hundred miles from here,' said Biggles.

'How are you going to get two hundred miles?'

'Well, I've a little petrol left in my tanks and I imagine the tanks of the machines I see over there aren't bone dry. Put it all together, and with what I have left I could get to Mosul. Even if I couldn't top up there I could get a message to Alex.'

'That's an idea,' said someone. 'I've had about enough of sitting here sweating. Our pay's overdue. The next thing we'll hear is there ain't going to be any more.'

Ginger wondered why the men hadn't thought of Biggles's suggestion themselves, but he gathered from the conversation that followed that not only were their three machines military types, which would be hard to explain in Mosul or anywhere else, but as a result of their several sorties they might be identified. It wouldn't be safe to land them anywhere except in their remote retreat. It was generally agreed, however, that the Beechcraft, being a civil type, might get away with it. It was too late to start for Mosul that day—or it would be by the time any remaining petrol had been transferred to the Beechcraft—so Biggles said if they'd do that he'd go in the morning. Meantime, somebody pointed out, the Douglas plane might arrive with Klein's successor—and some beer.

Ginger hoped fervently that it would not.

Now that there was something to do, the atmosphere of pessimistic resignation gave way to a less depressing mood all round. Biggles parted with most of his cigarettes. 'Where do we sleep?' he asked.

'You can please yourself whether you sleep in a tent and get sandfly fever or doss down in the castle with the snakes, scorpions and mosquitoes,' he was told.

Biggles said they would go to the castle. It should be cooler than a tent. 'What about grub,' he asked.

'There's plenty of bully and biscuits in the wooden hut. Help yourself,' he was informed.

Collecting their kit from the Beechcraft they walked on to the hut, a prefabricated structure that had evidently been flown out and assembled on the spot. Nobody went with them. The door stood wide open.

Biggles took one step over the threshold and then stopped, staring at the litter inside. It was plain that this one weatherproof building was the general store, workshop and armoury. Broken packing-cases lay around. Tools were flung anyhow on a bench. Spare parts, oil and petrol drums were piled in heaps. Some small bombs, explosive and incendiary, lay in a corner. But what delighted Ginger were some weapons, rifles and pistols, that hung at all angles, on nails, on the walls, over more broken packing-cases, this time of ammunition.

'Just take a good look,' invited Biggles grimly. 'And I've heard fellows in the services wondering why discipline is necessary! This is what happens when there isn't any—when a bunch of men are left to themselves. It's nobody's job to do anything, so everybody does nothing. Is anybody watching us?'

'No.'

'Then we'll have a couple of Lugers and some ammunition. Imagine it. Even in a place like this these fools haven't the wit to post a guard. I know what'll happen here one day. I can only marvel that it hasn't happened before.'

'What?'

'I'll tell you presently. We mustn't be too long. Grab a gun. We'll take some rations, too.'

Presently, heavily laden, they walked on towards the castle, a matter of only a few hundred yards away.

'A pretty rotten lot,' was Ginger's verdict of their new comrades.

'Rotten maybe, but dangerous,' replied Biggles. 'When we arrived they were about ripe for mutiny. I suspect some of them would have pushed off had they anywhere to go, and any way of getting there. What they may not realize is—and I'm pretty sure I'm right in this—they'll never get out. The Committee will see to that. The old saying, dead men can't talk, is still true. That could be one of the reasons why this place was chosen for a hide-out. All the surviving members of the Committee have to do is withhold petrol— when it suits them—and these poor fools have had it. There's no walking home from the Valley of the Tartars.'

'That goes for us.'

'I realized that before I landed. I must admit I was a bit shaken when they said there was no petrol. I relied on there being plenty here, so we could fly out when it suited us. That's why I've put forward this scheme of going to Mosul. I shan't come back, of course. I've seen all I want to see here. Some of these fellows will rat on each other when they're questioned by the police, to save their own skins. They always do.

So the whole racket will be exposed. There's only one snag now to get over.'

'What's that?'

'I still don't know what country we're in, so who's going to handle the job? To bring it before an international court would mean argument, and argument means delay—during which time the wise guys at the top would pull their irons out of the fire and get away with it. However, that'll come later. The thing is to get away from here, and the sooner the better. I don't like the idea of this Douglas being available in Alex. Von Stalhein might decide to use it. There's a pilot there, too—this fellow Liebnitz.'

'What did you mean about these fellows being crazy not to post a guard?'

'Had any of them served in the R.A.F. they'd know. The Kurds, some of the wildest tribes on earth, live in these hills. Like the Pathans and Wazirs on the North-West Frontier they've lived for thousands of years by raiding the people of the plains. That's their life—business and pleasure combined. They pinch anything, from camels to corn, but the most valuable loot of all is weapons and ammunition. They can't get those any other way; but they must have them to raid, and they must raid to live. Once upon a time they relied on speed to get back to the hills before they were overtaken. But they weren't fast enough for aircraft. Some years ago, when we took care of Iraq, our chaps caught them in the open, and so taught them that the good old raiding days were over. The R.A.F. is no longer here, but you can bet the Kurds haven't forgotten what happened when they were. They hate aircraft, and with good reason. One day they'll raid this place as sure as fate. They would probably have done it by now had they realized what things were like here. There's nothing to stop them as far as I can see. That's another reason why I shall be glad to see the back of it.'

Ginger looked apprehensively at the stark, apparently dead hills that frowned on them from three points of the compass.

'Let's have a dekko at the castle,' said Biggles.

Chapter 13
A Castle Without a Name

Under ordinary conditions the castle would have interested Ginger immensely, particularly if he had known something about it. It interested him now—but not for academical reasons. Its time-weathered walls revealed its antiquity; but, now that he was close to it, it was the size of the place that fascinated him. He reckoned it covered a good acre of ground.

It was plain at first glance that the primary consideration of the architect had been defence. Everything else was secondary. The site itself had obviously been chosen to that end. On three sides the walls rose sheer from perpendicular rock faces. Even so there was not a window—if occasional narrow slits could be called windows—less than thirty feet from the ground.

There was only one approach to the single entrance. This was a stone arched bridge over a ravine, just wide enough for one man to cross at a time. There was no parapet. The ravine, about fifteen feet across, was not very deep, and looking down as they walked over Ginger saw, from the chaos of boulders at the bottom, that it had at one time been a water-course. Great boulders and detritus that had rolled down the hills through the ages also lay on all sides, although, by a curious chance, none had struck the bridge or it must have been carried away.

From the far side of the bridge, steps had been hewn in the rock to a doorway, again just wide enough to admit one man at a time. There was no actual door. In fact, as they discovered later, there was no wood in the place at all. As they mounted the steps to the entrance Ginger couldn't help wondering what tales the steps could tell if they could speak.

From the doorway Biggles turned and surveyed the scene with an eye to its military possibilities. 'At the period this place was built it must have been literally impregnable,' he remarked. 'Even now, with modern weapons, a determined garrison would take a lot of shifting. I doubt if archaeologists have ever seen it, or we should have heard something about it. It's a masterpiece of its kind. But then, as I said just now, this is bad country, and only an armed force would dare to push as near the hills as this without risk of annihilation. Only a siege would reduce the place. Now we can understand why, in ancient times, a siege could last for years.'

'The fellows said there was water inside.'

'There would have to be, or thirst would soon do what bows and arrows could never do. As a matter of fact, I don't think the country could always have been like it is now. After all, what is there to defend? Water once ran in that ravine, and it can't be far under the ground now, or it would be no use sinking a well. No. There was a time when this district must have been fertile. If there was water there would be vegetation. Like so much of the Middle East it dried up and died when the water fizzled out. This is what men can do to a country. They're doing the same thing now, in more countries than one.'

'Men?'

'Cut down your forests and there's no cool ground to bring down the rain. But that's not our worry now.'

A short spiral staircase led into what they thought must be the main chamber of the castle; the quarters of the rank and file of the garrison. In the middle was the well. Biggles picked up a piece of fallen masonry and tossed it in. It took only about three seconds for it to splash. Which was to be expected, for a modern rope and bucket showed that the men outside had drawn up their water by hand.

Other signs of their occupation were there in plenty—empty tins, cartons, cigarette ends and the like, as well as some mattresses thrown down against the walls, which showed that some of the men had sometimes slept there. The great hall was gloomy on account of the comparatively tiny window slits, but Ginger could see nothing of the snakes or scorpions that had been promised. On the whole, considering its age, the building was in a surprisingly good state of repair, inside as well as outside. Only in one or two places had the masonry cracked, and this, Biggles thought, was due to an earthquake.

Said Biggles: 'I'd rather sleep in here than in one of those tents. It is at least reasonably cool. Besides, should anything go wrong we should have a better chance in here than outside. One man could hold this place against an army.'

'Let's hope we never have to play Horatius holding the bridge*,' answered Ginger warmly. Walking over to one of the slits he could see the tent-dwellers withdrawing any petrol that was left in the tanks of their machines. He told Biggles. 'Are you going to explore this place?' he asked.

'No,' answered Biggles. 'We've other things to think about. We might have a look at what's at the top of those steps, in case we have occasion to use them,' he

* A long poem by Macaulay describes how the Roman soldier Horatius kept invaders from entering Rome in 500 BC.

decided, pointing to another narrow flight of steps that wound upwards from a corner.

Cobwebs proclaimed that the steps had not been used for some time, and Ginger, pulling them off his face, and at the same time watching where he was putting his feet, was not sorry when they reached the top, to find themselves in another large room, although not so big as the one below, with loopholed turrets in two of the corners. Here there was that curious musty smell one usually encounters in ancient buildings.

Going to the nearest turret Biggles, with his penknife, flicked into space a black scorpion that was crawling on the sill. 'They were right about those venomous little beasts,' he remarked. 'Watch where you put your hands. This is no place to get stung.'

There were two of the standard window slits in the turret. One looked out over the improvised airfield and the plain beyond, behind which the sun was sinking like a monstrous orange, flooding the desolation with a strange unearthly glow. The men could be seen working on the Beechcraft.

Leaving Biggles watching them Ginger turned to the other loophole, which overlooked the bridge and the boulder-strewn rising ground which, falling to the sandy floor of the valley, formed its boundary. All was stark dead wilderness. The only living thing in sight was an area of straggling camelthorn. Or so he thought, and would, no doubt, have continued to think, had not a slight movement caught his eye. Instantly his eyes focused on the spot, yet so perfectly did the object—which did not move again—merge into the colourless background, that it took him a minute to pick it up. Even then he was not sure if he was looking at the thing that had moved, much less discern what it was. The trouble was, he was looking at a scene without outline. Nowhere was there any rest for the eyes. Observation was not made easier by the quivering of the heat-soaked air near the ground. But as he stared he thought he could make out a shape, a shape in the rough form of a man lying prone, his head towards the airfield. He was still by no means sure that this was not imagination.

'Biggles,' he said softly. 'Come here.'

Biggles joined him.

'At two hundred yards, a large pointed rock, with a sort of little spike on top. The sun is just catching it.'

'I've got it.'

Ginger held out his arm at full length. 'At nine o'clock, two fingers away. Does that look like a man to you—a man lying on his stomach?'

Biggles raised his arm, squinting past two fingers.

'I thought I saw it move,' said Ginger.

'I think you're right, but I wouldn't be sure,' answered Biggles slowly. 'Yes, by James!' he went on quickly. 'He moved again! I saw him distinctly. He's looking round the side of a rock. He couldn't be seen from below. Here, we're slightly above him. He couldn't have seen us coming to the castle. But then, he wouldn't, being where he is. We needn't wonder who he is or what he's doing. He's a Kurd, and he's watching the camp. I don't see any others. Now you'll see the point of my argument a little while ago about those fellows being crazy. If the camp is being watched you may be sure there's something in the wind. And those fools down there don't even suspect anything. Where do they think they are—on Margate beach?'

'What are you going to do—if anything?'

'We shall have to warn them. They'll laugh in our

154

faces of course. Fools always laugh at what they don't understand, or don't want to believe. We'd better go right away. This isn't a place to stroll about after dark. I want to see how much petrol they've managed to raise between them. Hark! Can you hear something?'

'I can hear it all right,' returned Ginger lugubriously. 'It's an aircraft. Multiple power units. It's that confounded Douglas.'

'I can see it,' said Biggles. 'Just coming out of the sun, heading for the valley. That puts an end to any ideas about going to the camp.'

In silence they watched the aircraft land and taxi in. Four men got out.

'Pantenelli, Festwolder and von Stalhein,' said Biggles. 'The other fellow must be the transport pilot we were told about. By thunder! Lindsay was right when he said those rascals would have to do their own dirty work for a bit. They haven't wasted any time.'

'They'd have to know what the position here was like.'

'It'd be a joke if they didn't bring any spare fuel with them, wouldn't it? They'd find themselves in the same position as the rest of us.'

'They'd take the Beechcraft, in which case we should lose it.'

'If we didn't get it first.'

'They won't give us a chance. They saw us take off. Seeing the machine they'll know we're here. They'll ask where we are. The gang will tell them we're in the castle. They'll come over to winkle us out.'

'Not necessarily. They'll still think we're two new hands, recruited by Raban. They can't possibly know our names—our real names. I don't see how von Stalhein could have an inkling that we're on this job.'

'They'll come over to ask why we pushed off this morning without von Stalhein, you watch it.'

'We'll tell them what happened at the hotel.'

'Suppose von Stalhein comes?'

'Oh, if he comes over the cat will be out of the bag with one beautiful jump,' admitted Biggles.

'Here they come, the whole pack of 'em,' muttered Ginger. 'Von Stalhein is with them. That, I'd say, has torn it.'

'Not at all,' disputed Biggles. 'We won't let 'em in.'

Ginger was not impressed. 'How long can we stay here?'

'If it comes to that, how long can they stay there?'

'As long as they feel like it, as far as I can see.'

'Then you can't see very far. We've got the water supply. I'd wager a month's pay that those useless erks in the camp haven't a pint of water between them. If nobody was detailed to fetch water you can bet your sweet life nobody fetched any.'

'Maybe the Douglas brought some beer.'

'I hope it has. Let 'em drink it. They'll get thirsty all the faster. But if there is any liquid going Pantenelli and Festwolder will keep it for themselves. They're not used to going without anything. But we'd better get downstairs. We look like having to do the Horatius act after all. Von Stalhein's face should be worth looking at when he sees us.'

'We can't stall off that mob.'

'Can't we? You see. Watch what happens when they realize we've got guns.'

'You'll use them?'

'That's what they're for. Most people in the world have sound reasons for not wanting to be shot, and that goes for the gang down there. They all want to go on living. They'll all know that the first man who

156

sets foot on that bridge will die. They'll know it because I shall tell 'em so. And I shan't be bluffing. It's either them or us for the chop, and it isn't going to be me if I can prevent it. As no one will be in a hurry to die there'll be no rush to be the first man on the bridge. The two most potent motives on this earth of ours are love and money. There's no love in that crowd, and money's no use if you've got a bullet in your ticker*.'

By the time they had reached the head of the steps overlooking the bridge the gang was only about a hundred yards away. Von Stalhein, Festwolder and Pantenelli walked in front. Ginger hoped that the lone Kurd might cause a diversion, but if he saw what was happening he did not show himself. The party continued to advance in a purposeful way. So far none of them had seen Biggles leaning against a side pillar just inside the entrance doorway.

Strangely, perhaps, it was Von Stalhein who saw him first. He stopped, advanced a few paces and stopped again. All Biggles had said about his expression came true, and revealed that he had not suspected who was in the castle. His face, usually immobile, took on a look of incredulity. He said something to his companions, who also stopped. What he said could not be heard, but that Biggles was the subject of the conversation was plain.

After a while the advance was resumed, but very slowly now, as if von Stalhein was feeling his way cautiously to find out what sort of reception was waiting for him.

Biggles allowed him to get nearly to the far side of the bridge. Then he called. 'That's close enough.

* Slang: heart.

157

What a fellow you are for changing jobs. I never know where I'm going to run into you next. Fancy meeting you here, of all places.'

'Do you intend to stay there,' asked von Stalhein.

'I've no intention of coming out.'

'We can talk about this.'

'You can talk from there. I'm listening.'

The chief members of the party on the far side of the bridge went into a huddle.

A wild thought occurred to Ginger that this was their chance to drop to the ground on the far side of the castle and make a dash for the Beechcraft, using the rope at the well for getting down. But he had to abandon the plan when, measuring the size of the loopholes with his eye, he saw that neither he nor Biggles could get through. The intention of the architect was, no doubt, that nobody should get in.

From their gesticulations, and the way they looked at the bridge, it seemed that those on the far side were contemplating an attack. Biggles squashed it by giving his assurance that the first man to step on it would never take another. He held up his Luger to let them see he was armed.

As there was no cover, and at such a range Biggles could hardly miss, no one volunteered to lead a storming party. Moreover, darkness was now fast closing in, so apart from bullets, the project offered some natural risks.

The men stood talking for some time. Then two were posted as guards and the rest retired towards the camp. They were soon lost to sight in the gathering darkness.

'So they're not going to try to get in,' observed Biggles.

'But they've seen to it that we don't get out. They'll

think up something and come back in the morning. They won't just leave us here.'

'By morning they'll be getting thirsty and be asking us for a drink,' asserted Biggles. 'Tomorrow will be another day, anyhow. We'll take it in turns to watch, and snatch a nap.'

'Can you see any way out of this?' asked Ginger.

'Frankly, no,' answered Biggles. 'The thing will just have to work itself out. If we can't stay here indefinitely neither can they stay there.'

'What about Algy? He might do something. He knows where we are.'

'Without an aircraft it's hard to see what he could do. Whatever he did would take time, and where we're concerned that's likely to be in short supply. Tomorrow will probably see the end of this business. Since there's nothing we can do about it ourselves let's leave it like that for the moment.'

Chapter 14
Outsiders Take a Hand

The night that followed was as strange as any that Ginger could remember. There was something unreal about it. The silent, brooding land, the brilliant moonlight and the black shapeless shadows cast by it, induced an uneasy feeling that he was no longer in the world he had always known but in a world in which life had yet to appear—or from which all life had departed. He wasn't sure which. It was such a world as might appear in a dream, a world peopled only by the spirits of a long-forgotten past. There was something frightening about it. For this the Biblical associations of the place may have been partly responsible. Certainly names that had not occurred to him since childhood passed in solemn procession before his eyes. Where were all these people now, men and women who had been so important in their day? Where were the hosts of soldiers and slaves who had sweated and toiled to build this fantastic fortress; who had gazed on this same scene under the same impassive moon and glittering stars? Gone. Gone to dust. Gone as utterly as if they had never been. In the all-enfolding silence the thought hung on him like a weight.

For all the sultry heat being cast off by the sun-soaked stones a cold hand seemed to touch his spine, and he prayed for the light of day to banish these melancholy meditations.

Once or twice, at long intervals, sometimes near

and sometimes far, a stone, dislodged by a reptile or by the hand of time, would clatter down the hillside, making in the deathly hush a noise out of all proportion to its size. Once, afar off, a jackal howled. At least, he could think of nothing else it might be.

It was his watch when, at long last, the air shivered at the approach of another day. First the grey false dawn, causing the stars in the east to lose their lustre, then the pale pink and golden rays of the rising sun, touching the dome of heaven above his head.

The voice of one of the guards on the far side of the bridge, asking for a drink of water, brought him back to the world of stern realities. He thought it was a strange request, and he was considering it when Biggles, who must have heard, appeared with the bucket in his hand.

'Come and get it,' he said. 'We'll call a truce for five minutes. No tricks.'

The man—it was the youngish pilot who had declared that he had had enough of the Valley—made a business of putting his gun on a rock before crossing the bridge, and, tilting the bucket, drank thirstily. 'Thanks,' he said, and after taking a step as if to withdraw, hesitated. 'You know what they're going to do?' he said softly.

'No,' answered Biggles.

'They're going to pull out. They say this place is finished. They're going to burn everything and then take everyone back to Alex. in the Douglas.'

'Leaving us here?'

'That's the idea. They know you can't get out. I thought I'd tip you off in return for the drink.'

'Thank you. What about the other machines?'

'They're going to burn 'em. They're about done, and they're getting a bit too well-known for our job, anyhow. We've no real maintenance equipment here, as you may have noticed. So long, and thanks a lot for the drink.' The man went back over the bridge, and picking up his gun, sat down behind a rock.

Biggles looked at Ginger. 'So that's the plan. I didn't think of it. Of course, I wasn't thinking of them burning the place up, or the machines. They know as well as we do that they couldn't take this place without casualties and it would take too long to starve us out. They'd run out of water, anyway.'

'Are they right in supposing we couldn't get out?'

'Quite right. It would be a hopeless proposition. An Arab, properly equipped and knowing the desert tracks, might do it. But not us. By noon the sand would burn the soles off our feet.'

'Look!' Ginger pointed towards the camp. 'Here they come.'

Some, not all, of the camp dwellers, appeared in the growing light, walked briskly towards the castle. Von Stalhein was with them. Pantenelli and Festwolder followed slowly. The remainder of the men were scattered about the camp doing one job or another—presumably getting ready for departure.

'What are they coming here for?' asked Ginger, watching the advancing party.

Biggles shrugged. 'I haven't a clue. Maybe they hope to pull a trick to knock us out. They'd rather bump us off, if they could, than leave us here, you may be sure.'

The rim of the sun was now showing above the horizon, turning the eternal sands to lakes of living gold. The air sparkled, but the awful silence, the silence that only the desert knows, persisted.

Biggles and Ginger, from a safe position just inside

the entrance archway, watched, prepared for anything except what actually happened.

It began with a gunshot near the camp, a hard yet flat report that echoed from hill to hill. A man who had been walking towards the wooden hut stumbled and fell. Then, as if the shot had been a signal, the silence was shattered and the wilderness came to life. Shots, shouts and yells, filled the air. In a moment, where all had been peace, all was confusion.

'Kurds,' said Biggles.

Ginger said nothing. He had nothing to say. Dazed by the sudden turmoil he could only stare.

What was happening in the camp itself he did not know. He could see men running about. Sometimes one would fall. The others took no notice. It seemed at first as if some of the men were trying to reach the wooden hut where the weapons were stored; but they were met by a fusillade of shots, whereupon the survivors turned about and fled towards the Douglas, which was standing some distance off, presumably in the hope of escaping what was obviously going to be a massacre. They never reached it. Out of a defile in the hills swept a compact band of horsemen, waving swords, galloping like madmen. These were the first Kurds Ginger had seen. Within a minute they cut down the running men and were tearing on towards the camp.

Never was a surprise onset more successful. It was evident that any survivors in the camp hadn't a hope of life.

The effect of the first shot on those near the castle had been to cause them to halt. Then those who were behind made the natural but fatal mistake of running towards the camp. Among these were Pantenelli and Festwolder. Not one reached it. Shots rang out from the hillside. Festwolder was one of those who fell. The rest turned again and raced for the castle. But they had left it too late. Wild-looking figures appeared between them and their objective. More shouts, more shots, and it was all over.

By this time von Stalhein, and another man who had been with him, had nearly reached the bridge, where the two who had been on guard were standing in an obvious state of indecision. It seemed to Ginger that they were all doomed, for, although they were unaware of it, more bearded, turbaned tribesmen, their sand-coloured robes tied up round their hips, were leaping down to intercept them.

'We'd better take a hand,' said Biggles, and raising his Luger he fired at the leader.

Von Stalhein spun round at the shot and looked at Biggles as if he thought he had fired at him; but Biggles shouted: 'Mark! Above you! Keep going. I'll try to hold 'em off.' To Ginger he muttered, as he opened fire: 'Get cracking.'

With two pistols picking them off the Kurds dived for cover and started shooting at the doorway, forcing Biggles and Ginger to a less exposed position. However, this relieved the pressure on the four white men. Three of them, dashing from cover to cover, and taking snap shots, were nearly at the bridge. Von Stalhein, not in the least flustered, moving more slowly, covered their rear, coolly and deliberately firing at any Kurd that showed. Near the bridge he stopped behind a rock, as if he had decided to make his last stand there.

'Keep going,' shouted Biggles. 'Come over here.'

The three men with von Stalhein needed no second invitation. They appeared to be out of ammunition, anyway, for one of them flung his pistol at the head

164

of a Kurd who came charging down on him. One of his companions dropped the man, and then all three made a rush for safety. Biggles let them through and then emptied his gun at the enemy as von Stalhein walked across.

'Good morning,' greeted Biggles, smiling curiously. 'You seem to be having a spot of bother outside.'

'Have you any Mauser cartridges?' asked von Stalhein.

'Only Luger—and I've only a ten packet of those,' replied Biggles, reloading.

'The camp's going up in flames,' reported Ginger.

'What about the machines,' asked Biggles.

'Burning,' Ginger told him laconically.

A lull followed. Ginger announced that the Kurds who had been near the castle were running towards the camp, possibly to celebrate the victory or more likely to join in the looting.

For a minute or two from the windows they watched the quarters of the secret squadron, and its equipment, going up in flames. Clouds of smoke rolled into the sky. There was a diversion when with a cracking explosion the bombs in the burning wooden hut blew up, bringing to an abrupt end the war dance of some Kurds who were performing near it. They may not have noticed the bombs there; or perhaps they didn't recognize them for what they were.

One of von Stalhein's men exclaimed joyfully at this, but Biggles shook his head. 'It won't make any difference,' he said.

'How many of them are there?' asked von Stalhein. 'You were in a better position to see than we were.'

'No fewer than two hundred, for a rough guess. Anyway, too many for us to handle,' averred Biggles. 'And by the way,' he went on, 'since we seem to have plenty on our plate without fighting each other may I take it that our hostilities are suspended until further notice?'

This was agreed, by the three men promptly, but by von Stalhein after a momentary hesitation.

'I'm sorry to put you in the embarrassing position of having to be helped by people whom you were hoping to liquidate, but that's the way things happen in this cockeyed world,' Biggles told him. 'Have you any cigarettes on you? Your toughs smoked most of mine yesterday—due to your firm's oversight in letting stocks here run out—and I smoked my last at daybreak.'

Von Stalhein produced a gold cigarette-case, opened and offered it. There were two cigarettes in it. Biggles took one. Von Stalhein took the other and fitted it carefully into the long holder he habitually used.

'I hope we're better off for cartridges,' said Biggles.

Von Stalhein said he had one only. The other three men had none between them. They had emptied their guns and carried no spares. Biggles had ten. Ginger seven.

'We shall have to be careful,' observed Biggles.

'Who are these people—Kurds?' questioned von Stalhein. Not for a moment did his stiff austerity relax.

'I imagine so,' answered Biggles. 'We spotted one lying on the hill watching the camp last evening, just before sundown. As a matter of fact we were just going down to warn the camp that something might be cooking when you arrived. In the circumstances we thought we had better stay where we were.'

'Very wise.'

'This raid has probably been projected for some time,' went on Biggles. 'The annoying thing—from your point of view—is that it wouldn't have happened had you arrived twenty-four hours earlier, because as a soldier you'd have had the sense to put the place in some sort of position for defence. When we arrived there were no guards. The armoury door was wide open. Having no guns on us we just helped ourselves. As it turned out, that was just as well. But it looks as if you're out of a job again. At least, you won't work for Pantenelli and Festwolder again.'

'Did you see what happened to them?'

'They were shot. If the shots didn't kill them they will have had their throats cut by now.'

Von Stalhein drew thoughtfully on his cigarette. 'What is going to be the end of this?'

'Your guess is as good as mine. The end of us, probably. The Kurds know we're here. They know we've lost our transport so they know we can't get out. That's why they're in no hurry. They also know we're in no state to stand a siege for any length of time.'

'Do I take it from that you are not expecting reinforcements?'

'You do.'

'Usually you have a card up your sleeve,' said von Stalhein drily.

'On this occasion my cards are all on the table.'

'What about Lacey and Lissie?'

'The last time I saw them they were in Alexandria.'

'Did they know you were coming here?'

'Yes—more or less. But they've no way of getting here, and if they had I don't see what they could do against this mob of fanatics. In the ordinary way, when the Kurds make a raid, when they've got what they want they beat it back to their hills where no one can follow. That's how it was when the R.A.F. was here.

167

What things are like now, under the Iraqis, I don't
know. My guess is that the Kurds will leave some men
here to winkle us out of this, or starve us out. One
tin of bully and half a dozen biscuits won't go far
between six men. There is this about it. There's
nothing we can do, so we needn't crack our brains
trying to think of something.'

'It isn't often you say that.'

'This is one of the rare occasions when I do.'

Silence fell.

From a turret window Ginger watched clouds of
smoke drifting into the pitiless sky. All that remained
of the aircraft were the metal members and some
smouldering debris.

Overhead, the sun toiled its daily course across the
heavens, regardless of the cares and follies of men.

The day dragged on. Those in the castle had
nothing to do but watch the Kurds cleaning up the
camp. It was, thought Ginger, a queer end to their
assignment, to stand watching a horde of barbarians
doing what they themselves had set out to do—and
doing it effectively. The squadron and its leaders were
finished. Even more remarkable was it to be in the
same room, for the first time ever, with von Stalhein,
without hostility by word or action on either side. It
was, he reflected, just one of those things . . .

It was late in the afternoon when a sudden burst of
activity among the Kurds took everyone to a window.
There appeared to be no reason for it, but it was
apparent from the general agitation that something
had happened. Men were running about with bundles
of loot. Horsemen were trying to steady, while they
loaded, mounts which had become restive, as if sens-
ing danger.

But within two minutes the explanation was forthcoming. Faintly through the shimmering air came the drone of an aircraft which the Kurds must have heard before those in the castle. Presently it appeared.

'Dragon*,' said Biggles, identifying the machine.

'Algy,' cried Ginger.

'Could be. If the machine was heading anywhere but on a straight course for the Valley I'd say it was an aircraft of one of the air companies operating over Iraq. It still could be. Some still use Dragons. The pilot could have come to see what the smoke was about. Whoever it is, I hope for his sake that he doesn't try to get down. If he does, he's had it. The Kurds probably take it for a military job. They wouldn't know the difference.'

'The pilot will guess what has happened, or seeing all those men, will surely have more sense than to land,' opined von Stalhein.

This view was soon confirmed. The Dragon made a circuit of the valley at about a thousand feet. Then it dropped down to five hundred, did another circuit and finished by diving low over the Kurds, who scattered. The pilot, apparently satisfied with his reconnaissance, climbed back to his original altitude and stood away to the west. The drone faded.

'Whoever it was,' said Biggles definitely, 'he's gone away quite sure of one thing, and that is, there isn't a living European in this valley.'

No one answered.

---

* A De Havilland *Dragon*, built in the 1930s. A twin-engined bi-plane aircraft carrying 4–6 passengers.

Chapter 15
Algy and the Dragon

As a matter of fact Algy *was* flying the Dragon. And when he turned away he *was* quite sure that if Biggles and Ginger were in the Valley of Tartars they were no longer alive. There was never any doubt in his mind about that. He knew from R.A.F. pilots who had served in Iraq the methods of the Kurdish hillmen with their captives.

What had happened was this.

In accordance with Biggles's final instructions in Alexandria, Algy had gone to the airport and Bertie had gone to the docks. At the airport the Beechcraft stood in plain view, and Algy was watching Biggles and Ginger to make sure they got safely away when a Rolls pulled up near him and, to his consternation, he saw von Stalhein step out. There were two men with him, but with those Algy was not concerned. Von Stalhein was enough, and from the way he ran out to the tarmac it was clear that he would have stopped the Beechcraft taking off if it had been possible. It was not, so Algy had a respite from his alarm when he saw the machine in the air. Even then he did not realize that von Stalhein had intended to be a passenger in the machine.

Withdrawing to a prudent distance he followed the proceedings with interest. During this period a steward passed the group, and in doing so touched his hat. Algy intercepted him, and under the pretext of looking for a friend asked the steward if he knew the names of the gentlemen who he had just saluted. The man told him that two were Mr. Festwolder and Mr. Pantenelli, both well-known at the airport, which they used frequently. The other he did not know. Thus Algy gathered another piece of important information, although it did nothing to ease his anxiety on Biggles's account.

Continuing to watch he saw the three men go into a hangar, from which, presently, a Douglas D.C. was pulled out and taken to the servicing station. Again Algy questioned an airport employee without success. The Douglas, he learned, was the property of Mr. Pantenelli, who used it to travel round his several commercial undertakings. He had just ordered the tanks to be filled for that purpose. A fourth person who had joined the group Algy took to be the pilot.

It did not take Algy long to arrive at the fairly obvious conclusion that von Stalhein, having missed his plane, was to be taken on in the Douglas. He did not realize that the other two men were going until they stepped into the machine. That was some time later. They had gone off in the Rolls, and Algy assumed that they would not be coming back. He watched the Douglas being serviced and tested. He was surprised when the Rolls returned, and its occupants rejoined the machine. It now looked as if all three were going, and this, at the end, proved to be the case.

The knowledge of what would happen when the plane landed at the Valley of Tartars, with Biggles and Ginger there, threw Algy into a flap, and finding a taxi he tore off to find Bertie to make him acquainted with the dangerous situation that had arisen. This he did.

Bertie said that there was only one thing to do, and

that was to get another machine and follow. But this, as they discovered when they got to the airport, was easier said than done. For the first time they were without a machine of their own, and never had they so badly needed one. Not for love or money would anyone allow them to borrow or hire an aircraft, which in the circumstances was not surprising.

'There's only one thing left,' declared Algy. 'We shall have to go to the Canal Zone*, tell the Air Officer Commanding what has happened and ask him to lend us a machine.'

'No use, old boy,' said Bertie despondently.

'Why not?'

'In the first place it will take hours to get to the Canal Zone, and the senior officer isn't likely to let us have an aircraft without getting the necessary authority. By that time, even if it came off, the Douglas will have come back and Biggles and Ginger will have had it.'

They were still debating the possibilities when an Air France liner, coming in from the west, landed, and one of the first people to step out of it was Marcel. They made a rush at him and asked him if he knew of any way of getting his hands on an aircraft. It didn't matter what sort as long as it had a range of 1,000 miles.

Marcel, naturally, wanted to know what all the fuss was about, and it took some time to tell him. He then dashed their hopes by telling them that he had no more idea than they had where an aircraft could be found. Had they been in France, yes; but Egypt was not France.

* The land surrounding the Suez Canal, controlled by the British until 1956.

'It isn't England either,' muttered Algy heavily.

Marcel said he was willing to go to the French Consular office to see if anything could be done. He pointed out that whatever they did they wouldn't get to the Valley of Tartars that day. This was so evident that Algy didn't argue about it. 'We'll go tomorrow,' he said. 'I'll go if I have to pinch a plane. I'm not going to sit here doing nothing.'

In the end it was agreed that Marcel should do everything in his power to get an aircraft. Algy and Bertie would go to their hotel, send a cable to the Air-Commodore requesting authority to requisition an aircraft, get their kit, pay their hotel bill and return to the airport in the morning. Marcel was to meet them there.

This arrangement went according to plan, although up to the time of their meeting, no reply had been received from their signal to London.

One look at Marcel's face was enough to tell Algy that he had not been successful. With an expressive shrug of resignation Marcel said he had been unable to do anything. Everything was cluttered up with red tape. He had, however, brought along some maps, made by the French Air Force in Syria, which he thought might be useful.

'They're a lot of good without an aircraft,' growled Algy.

The truth was, he—and Bertie, of course—was worried sick about the appalling situation that had arisen, and irritated by their helplessness to do anything about it.

They were still standing there talking when a Dragon landed. One man got out. Algy sprang to his feet, staring incredulously. 'I don't believe it,' he said in a dazed voice. 'It isn't true.'

173

The man was Air-Commodore Raymond.

Algy hailed him.

The Air-Commodore, seeing them, changed direction and strode towards them. And there was something about his step, and his expression, that made Algy, who had started to walk towards him, slow down.

The Air-Commodore came up. 'What do you fellows think you're doing,' he rapped out.

'Well sir, I—er—' stammered Algy, nonplussed by this brusque greeting.

'I thought you came out here to stop wars, not start them.'

'But we haven't started any wars,' protested Algy.

'It sounds mighty like it to me,' came back the Air-Commodore grimly.

'What have you heard?'

'A man named Lindsay came to see me. Not satisfied with leaving a trail of dead men behind you it is now proposed to launch a major offensive in the territory of a friendly country.'

'I don't think you've got it quite right, sir. I—'

'Where's Bigglesworth?'

'He's somewhere in Iraq, or Persia—to tell the truth, sir, I'm not quite sure where he is. But wherever he is it's doubtful if he's still alive. Hebblethwaite was with him. May I ask how you got here so quickly, sir?'

'When I heard Lindsay's story I decided it was time I took a hand. I was lucky to catch a Comet*, with a spare seat, bound for South Africa. It didn't stop at Alexandria, but at Cairo. So I chartered this Dragon there intending to look for you, either at your hotel or, as seemed more likely, in gaol.'

---

* A DeHavilland Comet, the first commercial jet-powered passenger aircraft. In service worldwide between 1952 and 1980.

'I cabled you last night for instructions, sir, but didn't get a reply.'

'I was on my way by then.'

'May we have that Dragon, sir?'

'What do you want it for?'

'I think I'd better tell you what's happened,' said Algy. And there, on a seat in the waiting-room, he gave the Air-Commodore a resumé of events up to date.

The Air-Commodore heard him out, and when he next spoke his tone of voice was less critical. 'Yes,' he said. 'I agree. The position is pretty desperate. I didn't realize it until now.' He looked at Marcel. 'You certainly started something, my lad. When I came here I was only concerned with preventing this business from starting an international rumpus. Or, for that matter, a national one. Apart from half a dozen countries protesting at the violation of their territory, if a word of this gets into the Press there will be a fine old row. You know how it is. People will snap off at the handle and accuse government officials of co-operating with the racketeers, and all the rest of it. Every country in the Middle East is ready to blow up. It only needs a spark. But never mind about that now. We must do something about Bigglesworth. He must have been out of his mind to go to this Valley place.'

'You know how he is, sir,' protested Algy. 'He won't accept hearsay evidence. To complete his case he wanted to see things for himself.'

'What did you intend to do if you could get an aircraft?'

'Fly to the Valley of Tartars and pick up Biggles and Ginger—if they're still alive.'

'It sounds a crazy proposition to me but we shall

175

have to try it,' said the Air-Commodore simply. 'I'll come with you. Do you think you can find this place?'

'I think so, sir. Marcel has some good maps.'

'Very well. We'll start right away. While the tanks are being topped up I'll ring the company that owns the Dragon and tell them what I'm doing. I'd also better have a word with Sir George Graham, the British *Chargé d'Affaires* in Cairo. Get everything ready.' The Air-Commodore went off.

That was how it came about that a rather ancient Dragon arrived, later in the day, over the smouldering ruins of the secret squadron in the Valley of the Tartars. And it may be said here that Algy had some difficulty in finding the place. Indeed, it is unlikely that he would have found it had it not been for the tell-take smoke, for the Air-Commodore had just given him orders to make for Mosul when it was noticed.

A few minutes later the aircraft was over the valley.

There had been some conjecture as to what was causing the smoke. The valley answered the question. What had happened was plain to see, and while Algy made his reconnaissance nobody spoke.

Then the Air-Commodore said: 'So the Kurds are up to their old tricks again. If von Stalhein didn't shoot Bigglesworth the Kurds will have done so—and everyone else in the valley by the look of things. I think we can abandon hope of seeing any of them alive. Queer that after all these years Bigglesworth and von Stalhein should go out together. All right, Lacey. Head for Mosul.'

'How about going down to see if—'

'Don't be ridiculous,' interrupted the Air-Commodore. 'What do you think we could do against that mob?'

Algy, looking down, knew in his heart that the question could be answered in one word. Nothing. Had he been alone with Bertie he would probably have landed, in which case they would certainly have lost their lives. As it was, the Air-Commodore and common sense prevailed.

Reluctantly he turned the nose of the Dragon towards Mosul, the Nineveh of the Old Testament, of which the Prophet had so truly said, it would one day be cast down, and dry like a wilderness. For the great walls that once took an army three days to march round, only a few crumbling stones, protruding from the sands, remain.

Chapter 16

A Strange Alliance

Those in the castle had watched the Dragon disappear over the horizon with sinking hopes. At least, Ginger had, for with its departure, the brief promise of relief that it had brought, went with it. He did not know who was in the machine, but whoever it was could not be blamed for keeping a safe distance between himself and the smoking ruins below.

On seeing that the aircraft did not intend to launch any form of attack the Kurds slowed the speed of their movements, although most of them continued packing up the fruits of their victory. Some, on wiry desert ponies, galloped over to look at the castle, but while in the open took care to keep out of range. After a while a number of them, both foot and horse, went into a conference, as their actions plainly showed, to decide what should be done about the surviving white men in the castle.

Biggles remarked: 'The choice is between trying to winkle us out or leaving us to stew in our own juice. They know we can't get away.'

Said von Stalhein: 'They love fighting, these sons of dogs. They will try winkling.'

Said Ginger: 'I say they'll leave us to stew, leaving some men to make sure that we do.'

This prediction proved to be the correct one, for as the sun sank into the desert, some of the men, after putting their horses out of sight in a *wadi**, took up positions on the hills, where they sat like vultures waiting for a stricken beast to die.

Biggles turned to von Stalhein. 'What do you want to do? Please yourself. I mean, you can ignore me.'

Answered von Stalhein, in his cold, unbending voice: 'Let us go out and kill some of these swine. I do not like the idea of sitting still waiting to die. Let us make it quick.'

'You go, if that's how you want it,' replied Biggles. 'Personally, I shall eat my share of our unconsumed rations and go to bed. Playing hide and seek over hot rocks with those stiffs isn't my idea of recreation. How do the men feel about it.' Biggles looked up.

The men made it clear in no uncertain terms that they agreed with him. They realized that they had to die, but saw no reason to hurry over it.

Von Stalhein bowed to the decision of the majority.

'We'll post guards,' Biggles told von Stalhein. 'We'll all take our turn. That should make it easy. To sit too long staring at these silent hills by night isn't good for any man.'

Watching from a loophole Ginger saw some Kurds moving farther along the building. There they stopped to look at something, but he couldn't see what it was.

Guards were arranged. Biggles drew the first watch. The rest disposed themselves about the floor according to their fancy.

Ginger, physically tired and mentally exhausted by lack of sleep and the high-speed events of the past few days, knew nothing more until he awoke to see a moonbeam slanting diagonally through a loophole.

* A dry waterbed.

So bright was it that for a startled moment he thought it was the beam of a torch. How long he had slept he did not know but he knew that it must be near dawn, for he could see von Stalhein, who had the last watch, squatting like a graven image in the doorway overlooking the bridge, his back to the room. Ginger tried to go to sleep again, but to his annoyance he found himself getting ever more wide awake. And as he lay there, in a silence so profound that it seemed to beat on his eardrums, a feeling grew on him that all was not well. He could find no reason for this, but the stirring of a dormant instinct, for certainly the conditions were ideal to arouse one if such a human faculty were still alive.

Half raising himself on an elbow he looked around. The others were sleeping. They might have been dead for all the movement they made. Only von Stalhein was awake, and in him he had the utmost faith, for whatever else he might be he was a soldier, whose early training had been at a school that had its foundations in iron-like discipline. No one would pass that doorway, he knew, while the Prussian ex-officer had breath in his body.

He lay back, and was half-way to sleep when a sound jerked him back to full wakefulness. It was only a slight rustle, no more than the hard dry skin of a snake might make on the stone floor. In fact, he thought it might be a snake. At all events, his nerves were now at full stretch, and he abandoned all idea of sleep. He lay still. But he was listening with that intensity, as one sometimes does in the dead of night, as if all his faculties were concentrated in that one sense. Without being aware of it he was waiting for the sound to be repeated.

His eyes were open. They moved restlessly, probing

180

the darkest corners of the room. And these seemed all the darker by reason of the moonlit areas.

Suddenly his eyes switched. They came to rest on the narrow entrance to the spiral stairway that gave access to the upper storeys. Had something moved there or was it his imagination? He needed no telling that in conditions such as these imagination can play tricks, can make a fool of a man. Yes! Something had moved. What it was he did not know. All he could see was a vague shadow darker than the rest.

His hand closed over the cold square butt of his Luger. Very slowly he raised his hand, an inch at a time, until the muzzle covered the shadow. Then he waited. He had to be sure. Sweat stood out in beads on his face from the strain, but still he would not risk making a fool of himself by alarming everyone for no purpose. Von Stalhein would sneer.

Then the shadow moved, swiftly but noiselessly, and he saw a man appear as if by magic just inside the doorway, pressed flat against the wall. The Luger crashed. Ginger sprang up and fired again into the open doorway. Half blinded by the flashes of his pistol he shouted: 'Look out! They're here!'

For an instant, where all had been silence, pandemonium reigned as recumbent figures sprang to their feet groping wildly for weapons. Then a match flared. The little naked flame showed a wild, unkempt figure asprawl the floor.

'The door in the corner,' said Ginger crisply. 'Watch it. That's where he came from.'

Von Stalhein did not leave his post. 'What is it?' he asked.

'They're inside the building,' Biggles told him.

Von Stalhein called to one of the men. 'Watch that

181

bridge and don't take your eyes off it,' he ordered curtly, and came into the room.

Ginger, still covering the doorway, pointed. 'That's where he came in. I happened to be awake.'

'By thunder! A good thing you were,' muttered Biggles.

'I think there was another behind him but I'm not sure.'

'Would you like me to go up and investigate?' von Stalhein asked Biggles.

'No—thanks. We're few enough to hold off this mob as it is. Don't go near that stairway anybody but be prepared for a rush. Thank goodness it'll soon be daylight.' As he finished speaking Biggles put a match to an empty cigarette carton that he had picked up from the floor.

In its yellow light von Stalhein stepped forward and picked up a Luger pistol that had been thrown from the hand of the Kurd when he fell. It was fully charged. He also removed a bulging bandolier. 'That is better,' he said. 'He got these in the camp. Kind of him to bring them to us. I don't think we need this,' he concluded. Taking the dead Kurd by the foot he dragged him through the dust of the floor to the outer doorway and flung him out.

The others stood silent while the body went bumping with a clatter of stones to the bottom of the ravine. There was something about the action that fascinated Ginger, although it appalled him. In it, he thought, was revealed the difference between the Prussian and Biggles. Somehow he couldn't imagine Biggles doing that. Yet von Stalhein was fully justified. The man had come to kill them. Instead, he himself had been killed. It was desirable, if not essential, to dispose of the body, for in such heat it would soon become unpleasant. Von Stalhein had disposed of it by the only method possible; yet there was something about the way he did it that betrayed that streak of ruthlessness for which a certain type of Prussian is notorious. However, it was done.

Von Stalhein was still standing in the doorway surveying the scene outside. Suddenly he jerked up his hand and his pistol spat. Simultaneously a bullet struck the stonework an inch or two from his head and ricocheted round the chamber. 'I think I got him,' said von Stalhein, without emotion.

'Come inside,' ordered Biggles coldly. 'You're drawing their fire, and one man more or less in that crowd will make no difference to them. But one man less will make a difference to us.'

'So that is why you invited us in,' sneered von Stalhein.

Biggles's face hardened. 'Listen, Hauptmann von Stalhein,' he said stiffly. 'I have never seen any reason to regard you with affection but I have never expressed a wish to see you dead. You are at liberty to stay here or go outside, as you wish; you can go to the devil as far as I'm concerned; but while you choose to stay here you will take orders from me.'

Von Stalhein clicked his heels and bowed.

Biggles turned to the others. 'Whichever way they come they can only come one at a time. Von Stalhein, guard the outer doorway. Ginger, watch the inside one.'

The order was obeyed and an attentive silence fell.

Time passed. So slowly as to be almost imperceptible, the grey mysterious light of dawn crept through the ancient loopholes.

There was nothing to eat, nothing to do, after one of the men with what seemed an unnecessary amount of noise pulled up a bucket of water from the well.

After a while von Stalhein said: 'Excuse me, Bigglesworth; what are we waiting for?'

'For nothing in particular. There is a chance that the Kurds may go. There is a remote chance that we may be relieved. Should either of those things happen, if we are alive we shall profit. If we've thrown away our lives uselessly we shall not.'

'Relieved? By whom?'

'Two friends of mine. You know them. They know roughly where we are. By some means or other they will get here. On that you may rely. The only matter in doubt is *when* they will get here.'

'Surely the matter for doubt is *what* they will do when they come.'

'That, I'm afraid, we must leave to them.'

There was another interval of silence.

It was broken, first, by wild cries on the hillside, and then, a moment or two later, by the drone of aircraft.

'Here comes Algy,' said Ginger, striving to remain calm.

'If it is he, then he is not alone, for I can see six machines,' announced von Stalhein from the doorway.

The drone became a roar as the machines came on, and could presently be identified as Harts* of the Iraqi Air Force. Curiously, perhaps, no one appeared to guess their purpose; at any rate it was not remarked. Ginger had just decided that it was only a routine patrol when there came the scream of falling bombs,

---

* Hawker Hart. A biplane 2–seater light bomber, armed with two machine guns.

and a few seconds later the sticks were throwing up clouds of sand and broken rock. Then the air vibrated as the machines broke formation, and diving, weaved over the landing ground and the surrounding hill-sides. Machine-guns chattered.

Occasionally through the dust Ginger could see Kurds galloping towards the shelter of their mountains.

'Your friends seem to have gone to quite a lot of trouble,' said von Stalhein.

'Whether they were responsible or not, someone is making quite a spot of trouble for our enemies,' returned Biggles. 'Ah! Here comes that old Dragon. That explains it. I think we had better stay where we are for a little while.'

They watched while the Harts recovered formation and stood away to the west. The Dragon landed. Then, into the valley, slowly, rolled three armoured cars.

'That seems to be all,' said Biggles. 'Let's go down.'

'May I have your orders please,' requested von Stalhein, as coldly emotionless as ever.

'Oh, you'd better come with us,' answered Biggles casually. 'Our friends may have some cigarettes. I'm sure you can do with some. Anyway, I can.'

Keeping a watchful eye open for snipers they marched out of the castle and on to the landing ground.

Long before they reached the Dragon Ginger had recognized not only Algy, Bertie, and Marcel, but, to his unbounded amazement, Air-Commodore Raymond.

'Quite a family reunion,' observed Biggles whimsically. 'As they say, wonders will never cease.'

If Ginger was astonished to see the Air-Commodore it was no more than that of the others when they saw von Stalhein, as their expressions made apparent. Ginger realized, of course, that the rescue party didn't expect to find any of them alive; as in fact they were saying a few minutes later.

The Air-Commodore's face when Biggles introduced von Stalhein was a study. 'You've heard of this gentleman, sir, but I don't think you've ever actually met,' said Biggles, deadly serious.

'Yes . . . I mean no,' said the Air-Commodore, in a curious voice.

Biggles winked at Algy as von Stalhein clicked his heels and bowed stiffly from the waist.

'War certainly makes strange bedfellows,' averred the Air-Commodore, in a voice heavy with wonder. 'I don't know why you aren't all dead. You can tell me later.'

'Things were a bit sticky at times,' admitted Biggles. 'And the deuce of it was we hadn't a cigarette between us. Can anyone oblige?'

The Air-Commodore pulled out his case. After Biggles had taken a cigarette the Air-Commodore offered the case to von Stalhein with the remark: 'This is something I never expected to do.'

'And this, sir,' answered von Stalhein without a smile as he took a cigarette, 'is something *I* never expected to do.'

'I think we'd better get along to Baghdad,' stated the Air-Commodore. 'There will be a lot of explaining to be done.'

Chapter 17
Aftermath

So ended a case which provided Biggles and his comrades with material for argument and conjecture for many days to come. The war-mongering racket had been wiped out completely, but who had been responsible for it? To Marcel undoubtedly went the credit for realizing what was going on, but who had broken up the gang? A case could be made for several people—Biggles, Algy, Lindsay and even the Kurds. Biggles took the view that with the death of Klutz, the chief organizer, the thing would have gone to pieces anyway. Klein, the commander of the secret squadron, by his own folly had contributed largely to the breakup. Had he done his job properly the Kurds could not have done what they did. But, as Biggles said, there is always a weak link in a chain as long as the one organized by the Committee of Three. Had the French Air Force not been on guard when Voss had tried to steal a machine things would have fallen out very differently. And so the argument could be carried on indefinitely. All that really mattered was the war-makers syndicate was finished. With the death of the ringleaders the rank and file would inevitably break up when no more pay was forthcoming.

The Air-Commodore's explanation of the final phase was simple. When the Dragon had arrived over the Valley, and those in it had seen what was happening below, they had concluded, naturally, that every man had been massacred. The machine had gone to

Mosul, where the Air-Commodore had reported the raid, withholding his own particular interest.

The Iraqi Government, it transpired, knew there were people in the Valley of the Tartars, but was under the impression that they were prospecting for oil. Indeed, Klutz had obtained a concession for that purpose. Anyway, officials at Mosul had reported the raid to Baghdad, with the result that a punitive force had been sent out. This sort of thing, to them, was nothing new. They did not know, and may not know to this day, what was actually going on in the Valley. The Air-Commodore, maintaining his policy of silence, did not enlighten them, seeing no reason to do so now that the gang no longer existed. He, with the others, had returned to the Valley for no other purpose than to find and bury the bodies of Biggles and Ginger, not for a moment supposing they were still alive.

The Dragon finished its day's work at Baghdad, and there, at the Maude Hotel, arose the question of the disposal of von Stalhein and the surviving members of the Valley establishment. After some discussion with Biggles the Air-Commodore decided that there was no case against them. It was useless to surmise what von Stalhein would have done had he been given time and opportunity; the fact was, he had joined the gang just in time to witness its dissolution.

As for the others, what could be done with them? There was no evidence against them likely to impress a court of law, and they were not likely to provide it. All that would happen, if they were charged with anything, would be the exposure of the whole unsavoury business. That did not suit the Air-Commodore, who, still fearing political repercussions, thought it better to let sleeping dogs—and dead dogs—lie. So the men were allowed to go free, Marcel warning them that if ever they set foot on French soil they would be arrested as deserters from the Foreign Legion. He could not, of course, arrest them on foreign soil, and it was hardly worthwhile going through the long and difficult process of extradition. So statements, not to be used as evidence against them, were taken, and the men allowed to go. These statements were in due course filed with the reports of Biggles and the Air-Commodore.

Raban and Voudron, who were under arrest in French North Africa, were not so lucky. They were tried, and sent to prison, one for inducing legionnaires to desert, and the other for aiding and abetting him. The Villa Mimosa is now empty.

It may as well be said here that the murders in the Hotel Continentale were never regarded by the Egyptian police as anything but the work of an ordinary thief. What ultimately happened to the man responsible, Lindsay, was not known, for when the Scotland Yard party got back to London he had vanished. They never saw him, or heard of him, again.

Perhaps the most curious feature of the whole extraordinary finale, at any rate to Ginger, concerned von Stalhein. In spite of all that was known of his sinister activities and associations there was no case against him, either, for the simple reason that nothing could be proved. When Biggles asked him, as a matter of formality, what he intended to do, he replied, coldly, that he had the matter under consideration. Asked if they could give him a lift to Egypt, where they were going to return the Dragon to its owners, he said he was quite capable of taking care of himself. Was he free to do? he enquired. Biggles said yes. Whereupon he clicked his heels, bowed, turned abruptly and marched out of the hotel to mingle with the motley brown-skinned crowd taking the air after the heat of the day.

'A strange man,' remarked the Air-Commodore. 'I wonder what he'll do?'

'Oh, he'll find some mischief somewhere, no doubt,' replied Biggles. 'It seems to be one of the things he does really well.'

'He's had a lot of practice.'

'He also seems to be as good at getting out of scrapes—'

'As you do,' murmured the Air-Commodore, succinctly.

Today, in Biggles's private museum, there is a souvenir of this strange affair. It is a small buttonhole badge, and the device is an Oriental Lamp—the one, as Ginger says, they helped to put out.